KISSING DANGER

RUTHLESS EMPIRE

BOOK THREE

BY EVIE RILEY

Kissing Danger

An MM Mafia Romance

Ruthless Empire

Book Three

Copyright © 2024

Evie Riley

ISBN: 978-1-77357-656-5

978-1-77357-657-2

Published by Naughty Nights Press LLC

Cover Art By CDG Cover Designs

KISSING DANGER

Bright Lights and Scorching City Nights...

In the dazzling world of high fashion and finance, Deacon Millar, a talented clothing designer with dreams of making a name for himself, lands a coveted position working for the enigmatic billionaire, Nathan Sterling.

Amid the glamour of a chic industry gala, fueled by a mutual desire for success and an unexpected attraction, Deacon and Nathan succumb to a night of intense passion that forever alters the landscape of their professional relationship.

One night then becomes two, even while they both claim it won't become more than that, and then three, four, and more...

Caught in a whirlwind of forbidden love and a dangerous underworld, can Deacon and Nathan navigate the intricacies of their evolving relationship within the competitive world of fashion, finance, and the mafia? Or will their intense connection lead to a professional unraveling?

TWs: Murder and violence.

CHAPTER ONE

Deacon

It was one hour until show time, and the finale of my showcase was missing. An entire dress, which had taken me six months to create, had just completely vanished.

Panic was not the right word for what I was feeling. No. I was beyond panic. I had transcended to a whole new level of emotion never before experienced by humans.

The dress had been in its transport bag when I checked it this morning. I'd personally arranged each piece of my showcase on the hangers, in the order they would appear, along with the chosen accessories and decorations the model would wear.

Twelve ensembles remained exactly where I'd arranged them, but the last piece, the crown jewel of the collection meant to show off the height of my skills as a designer, was completely gone. Even the shoes and jewelry were missing.

Had someone stolen it?

It wasn't unheard of for fashion designers to sabotage each other, especially at such an important event that could make or break a designer's career, but why sabotage me?

It was my first high tier fashion event. I was only an up-and-coming designer with a tentative foot through the door. I wasn't a threat to anyone yet.

I didn't even count as competition. I'd earned a spot in the event by the skin of my teeth and a whole lot of luck. Originally, I'd been rejected, but another designer had dropped out at the last minute, and they needed a replacement immediately. I'd been one of the few who could fill the role with such short notice, mostly because I lived in the same city as the event.

KISSING DANGER

The backstage of a fashion show was a blur of chaos and fabric. Surrounded by so much activity, I stood immobile and stared at the empty rack where my grand finale piece should have been.

A cold wave of calm washed over me.

A long, manicured nail poked me in the shoulder. "So, what's the plan?" Kiki asked me. She'd only been my assistant for a few months, but she'd been my friend for a lot longer.

"Panic," I said without any inflection in my voice.

Kiki sighed and twirled a blonde ringlet of hair around her finger. "Okay. But then after that, what's the plan? I know you, Deke. You've always got a backup idea."

I shook my head. "If it was one of the other ensembles, we could throw something together or just leave it out entirely, but it's the finale piece. There's no way to..."

My gaze traveled toward a supply box off to the side that had been stashed under a table.

"The kimono."

Kiki pulled out the box, but she didn't look convinced. "It's not finished. The pieces are cut, but we scrapped the idea before stitching anything together. We only even brought it because we thought the brocade might make for a good accessory."

Together, the two of us spread the pieces of fabric over the table. A fashion showcase almost always ended with a large over-the-top dress. Often a wedding dress, but not always. I'd toyed with the idea of creating an Asian inspired robe, with a long hem and sleeves that would trail behind the model similar to a wedding train, but there hadn't been enough time to get it together and I already had a more traditional dress mostly made that would also fit the bill.

Now, the elaborately embroidered fabric sat in pieces on the table.

Kiki picked up one piece, holding it delicately between the points of two of her fingernails. "There's not enough time to stitch it together. This won't work."

I dragged a mannequin dress-form over to the table, along with my sewing kit.

"Let me worry about this. You just focus on getting the other models into their outfits and ready to go."

An hour was simultaneously a lot of

time and no time at all. After it had passed, the other models were all ready, and I showed Kiki what I'd managed to put together.

"That's not an outfit. Nothing's even stitched together."

"It's a deconstructed outfit," I said, indicating where the pieces of fabric were attached to the model by hidden strings and a few carefully placed stitches. "It's like when you go to a fancy restaurant and they serve something simple, like a burger, and present it deconstructed with all the ingredients separated. This is the same thing."

Her eyebrow hiked up so high it nearly disappeared into her hairline. "That's the kind of thing lazy chefs do when they want to charge more."

With a flourishing wave of my hand, I ushered the models into line. "Luckily, I am not a chef. I'm an artist. It's artsy. It'll work. Not like we have much of a choice anyway. Our turn on the runway is almost here. Let's go."

The *Costumes and Cars Fashion Show* was held every year during the spring fashion week at *The Hollywood Car Museum* in Las Vegas. While not the biggest fashion event in the world, it wasn't insignificant either. As I hung in the back wings, peering out between the curtains as the first of my creation-bedazzled models started walking down the runway, a flutter of nervousness attacked my stomach. There were so many important people sitting in the audience just a few yards away, watching my work pass by on the pseudo-catwalk with critical eyes. Whispering. Judging. Some of them could end my career with a single word.

Don't think about that.

Focus on the outfits.

The art.

The things I can control.

The runway was set up in a large showroom usually only dedicated to cars. Models walked from one end of the room to the other and back, illuminated by spotlights as well as the ambient light filtering in through the large windows that took up an entire wall. The room had a very industrial feel, with concrete and steel everywhere. All the cars on display had been moved to one side of the runway while the audience sat in chairs on the other, so the guests watched each model walk past a backdrop of gleaming classic automobiles.

Some of the fashion designers featured at the event had chosen to ignore the location and presented outfits that showcased their own personal design, while some designers had taken obvious inspiration from the location and presented car-themed creations. One noteworthy designer had presented a series of outfits inspired by the movies in which each of the background cars had appeared.

I'd chosen none of these options, and while I didn't think most people would get what my collection was supposed to represent, I was pleased to see that my designs at least didn't look out of place.

Model after model took their turn on the runway until it was time for the last one. The 'deconstructed' outfit I'd slapped together in an hour. As the model stepped out onto the runway, I crossed my fingers and held my breath.

It didn't move how I wanted. The long strips of cloth that would have made up the sleeves dragged along the floor. That wouldn't have been a problem if the sleeves were attached to the rest of the garment for support, but tied directly to the model's arms as they were, the model had no choice but to hold her arms steady and forcibly pull the fabric along. Every step looked like a battle fought and won.

However, all of the fabric stayed in place, and when the model finally finished her turn on the runway, she was still as dressed as when she'd started walking.

I breathed a sigh of relief. It was over. The whole showcase had been presented without any catastrophes or wardrobe malfunctions.

"What are you doing?" Kiki hissed at me. "Get out there and take your bow."

I was so overcome with relief that I almost forgot. All of the models gathered into a single line to give the audience one last look at the collection all together, and I was meant to go out with them.

The spotlights were so bright, I could barely see the audience as I stepped out onto the runway. I walked out to the middle and stopped right in front of the Lotus submarine car from the James Bond movies and took a bow in the audience's general direction. I couldn't hear what the announcer was saying over the pounding of my own pulse in my ears, and I just hoped that my smile looked suave instead of manic.

Then, I was back behind the curtains, and it really was over. As the next designer prepared for their turn in the spotlight, I collapsed into a folding chair back in my prep area and stared blankly at the wall.

"Well," Kiki said from where she stood beside me. "That could have gone worse."

I mutely nodded my agreement.

She watched me for a moment. "Do you need a moment to process?"

I silently nodded again.

She sighed, though not in an annoyed way. More like the resignation of someone who was right when they would have preferred to be wrong.

"All right. You sit there and decompress. I'll handle the wrap up and get everything put away. But you had better be back to functioning properly in time for the after party. You need to sweet talk the investors and make us some money. Try to land a contract. Maybe get hired by an important brand. You know, the whole reason why we're here."

Right. The banquet that always took place after these things was my least favorite yet the most important part of the night. The banquets I'd been to at smaller fashion shows were bad enough. At such a big event, I imagined it would be even worse.

Well, nothing to do but smile and act charming. I could do that. I didn't even have to be sincere. Just show up and say the right things.

The rest of the fashion show wrapped up, and soon enough, I found myself in a banquet hall full of important people, holding a glass of champagne I didn't actually like, and trying not to bump into anyone.

Small talk was one of my hard-won skills. It didn't come naturally, but enough time spent talking to clients as I brought their visions to life had made it a necessary skill to learn. Once I knew what to talk about, I could manage, but I could never figure out where to start.

That was where Kiki came in handy. She stayed at my side during the event, pointing me toward the right people while whispering in my ear about who they were, why they were important, and what topics they were interested in.

Why couldn't an artist just make art?

Why did I have to be a business and advertising expert as well, constantly marketing myself?

"All right, I think that went well," Kiki announced after I'd made my first pass around the room and shook two dozen different hands. "There's definitely some interest in your work. While I still don't agree with your last piece, people seem to like your 'deconstructed' outfit, so good job there."

I gave her an over-exaggerated bow. "I'm so glad Her Highness approves of this lowly peasant's work."

She retaliated by punching me in the shoulder. "Shut up and stop fooling around. Now, I'll give you a few minutes to take a break and get something to drink before I collect you again and we can focus on the more promising investors."

"You are determined to get me hired by a big-name label tonight, aren't you."

Quickly fixing her makeup in a compact mirror that she always carried around, Kiki gave me a wink. "Your career is my career, and I take my career very seriously. I wouldn't have accepted the job as your assistant if I didn't think you had the potential to make it big."

"Well, at least one of us has faith." I searched around the room and found the open bar not far away. "Now, you said I could have a drink, so I think the bar is calling my name."

"Only one drink," Kiki called after me as I walked away. "We need you sober tonight, so don't get drunk."

CHAPTER TWO

Deacon

There was a bit of a crowd around the bar, so it took me a moment to actually get a drink. Just a regular rum and coke. Nothing too hard so I didn't risk getting drunk; my alcohol tolerance was disappointingly low, and the caffeine would help me keep my energy up throughout the rest of the night.

People dressed in fancy suits and dresses pressed all around, laughing and bumping into one another. The heat of so many bodies in close proximity was making me lightheaded and I took a large gulp of my drink to try and cool down.

That was when I remembered that I'd eaten almost nothing the entire day, too nervous to choke down more than a few saltine crackers at breakfast. The alcohol hit my empty stomach like a sledgehammer and the room instantly began to spin. I stumbled and knocked into the person next to me, causing them to spill their drink.

"So sorry," I stammered as I stared down at the new puddle on the floor. Judging by the smell, it had been a very expensive brand of whiskey. It had also stained the person's shoes. Luckily, they were leather, so they should clean up easily, but I still winced. People in the fashion world tended to be very particular about their clothes, myself included, so I braced myself for yelling.

"If you flinch like that, people will think I'm going to hit you," a deep masculine voice said.

I couldn't tell if the man was angry or not. He had very little inflection in his voice, but at least he wasn't yelling. Feeling hopeful, I finally raised my gaze from the floor, but before I could get a good look at the man, he grabbed my arm just above the elbow and dragged me away from the crowd.

"Come with me."

My only choices were to either comply or make a scene. His grip didn't hurt, but it was too solid for me to slip away. For now, I decided to follow him, and would only resort to making a scene if he tried to remove me from the room altogether.

Luckily, he merely brought me to a more secluded corner where there was a bench for me to sit down. A cold water bottle was pressed into my hand, which the man had apparently snagged from the bar.

"Here. Drink something. You look like you're about to pass out."

"Thanks," I said, and winced when my voice cracked. "I'm just a bit overheated, and I didn't eat enough today. Nothing serious." The cap of the water bottle cracked when I twisted it open, meaning the seal hadn't been tampered with, so I gulped down the water with confidence that at least the stranger wasn't trying to drug me.

"Nervous for the show, I assume," he said as he watched me drink.

Glancing up to finally get a proper look at the man, I nearly choked on my water.

Working in the fashion industry, I'd built up a tolerance toward beautiful people. I was surrounded by them every day, and the delicate beauty that most models and fashionistas tended to prefer had never really interested me on anything other than an aesthetic level.

Rugged handsomeness, on the other hand, was woefully lacking in the fashion world, so I had no immunity to it. When I looked up at a man so perfectly "my type" that he could have been picked directly from my wet dreams, my soul nearly left my body.

Well over six feet, he was a perfect mix of rough and refined. His hair was short and immaculate, not a hair out of place, and his features were both broad and sharp. Even his more subjective traits, such as the gray hair at his temples and the tattoos I could see on his neck and the backs of his hands hit my preferences perfectly.

So, I had a weakness for older men and secret bad boys. A lot of people did. I wasn't ashamed of my preferences.

As if guessing where my thoughts had wandered, the man smiled. It was just a slight curve of his lips and didn't show any teeth, but I could tell the expression was genuine.

"Nathan Sterling," he said as he held out his hand.

I shook it, and winced when I realized condensation from the water bottle had left my hand unpleasantly damp. My words stuttered, refusing to come out properly. I needed to say something, but the ability to start a conversation had completely abandoned me.

"Deacon Millar," I eventually managed to blurt out.

"I know," he said as he took a seat next to me, politely refusing to wipe his hand free of the moisture I'd definitely left behind. "Your collection had that interesting piece at the end."

I couldn't help the snort that escaped me and quickly took another swallow of water. "Interesting is a word for it."

Up close, I got a better view of Nathan's suit, and my opinion of him rose even higher. A dark gray silk blend, it had a subtle herringbone pattern woven in, and had obviously been tailor made for him. Understated and classy, he didn't need to put on bizarre colors or patterns to stand out. The one odd detail I noticed was his cufflinks. The iron dark metal was stamped with an image of a wolf's head and lacked any other embellishment.

I realized I'd been observing his clothes a little too long when he tugged his cuffs back into place.

I quickly snapped my gaze back up to his face. Thankfully, he didn't seem annoyed. Rather, he seemed amused by my distraction.

"I'm guessing that wasn't what you originally planned to have as your finale piece."

Heaving a sigh, I explained about the missing dress.

"Even the model who was supposed to wear the dress is nowhere to be found. I'm hoping she didn't steal it." Feeling a little more confident now that I'd managed to string several sentences together without stumbling—and the dizzy spell had passed—I set the water bottle aside to face Nathan directly.

"How'd you know that last piece wasn't planned? Everyone I've talked to so far has been praising me for my 'artistic deconstruction of fashion'. I haven't had the heart to tell anyone I slapped it together at the last minute."

He laughed. A single sharp barking sound, like the snap of sharp jaws. "I thought it was obvious. The last piece didn't fit the theme of the rest."

"The... theme?" I asked, equal parts hopeful and wary.

"Yeah. Your pieces each embodied the movement of the different cars on display."

A spark of joy, and the thrill of recognition, filled me. Before I could second-guess myself, I slapped his arm like we were old friends, a big grin splitting my face.

"Thank you. Finally, someone gets it. Even my assistant didn't really get what I was going for."

Luckily, he didn't seem to mind the slap. Based on the muscle I'd felt under his suit, I wasn't sure he even noticed the impact of my hand.

"I wasn't sure at first," he admitted. "It was just a general observation that the first outfit seemed to match the low riding speed of one of the cars. It wasn't until the fourth outfit that I was sure about the theme. Making that poor girl walk in shoes of two different heights seemed a bit cruel, but it was a perfect representation of a really old classic car that has no shocks and can't get above thirty kilometers an hour."

His use of kilometers instead of miles alerted me to the slight accent in his voice. It was slight, and I couldn't place the country, but I was at least certain that he wasn't born in America.

Not that it mattered. He could have been a penguin from Antarctica for all I cared. I was just happy to have someone I could talk with about my art who actually understood it.

"I second-guessed myself so many times about using those shoes. I was terrified that the model would trip halfway down the runway, but the piece wouldn't move the same without that uneven gait."

Nathan merely shrugged and leaned back a little more, draping one arm over the back of the bench so it pressed against my shoulder. "The models are professionals. Walking under difficult conditions is their job. If they can't figure it out, then they should find a new job. But what made you choose that kind of theme? It seems a lot harder to capture than what everyone else chose to go with."

"Cars are meant to move," I said, getting excited enough that I was talking with my hands as much as my mouth. "They aren't meant to just sit in a showroom. Cars, even ones just meant for the movies, belong on the road. For speed and movement. To only admire their form when they're sitting still is like... like presenting a leather chair and calling it a horse."

With a few pointed questions from Nathan, I went into a long description of my artistic choices, my overall style and vision for my work, and how I'd put it all together. It was only when I found myself explaining the pros and cons of muslin that I realized how long I'd been talking.

"Oh my God," I gasped, checking my watch. "I've been babbling for twenty minutes. Why didn't you stop me? You must have been bored out of your skull."

Nathan's broad hand grabbed my wrist, hiding my watch from view. "I enjoy it when people are passionate about something. There's a depressing lack of passion in this world. Besides, I'm glad someone can appreciate the spirit of the cars here. That's why I chose to come to this event. I don't actually know much about fashion, but I know about cars, so I was hoping that would help bridge the gap. I was getting disheartened when I realized that the cars were just meant to be an aesthetic backdrop and not a feature of the event."

He looked around the room like he was searching for something, although I wasn't sure what he could possibly see through the crowd of people. "You know," he whispered to me. "This museum has a new exhibit where you can drive some of the cars. Not the one-of-a-kind ones from movies, but some of the standard classics. It's technically closed for this event, but I could probably convince the staff to open it if you'd like to join me."

My initial answer was "absolutely," but before I could say so, I caught sight of my watch again. So much time had passed while I'd been talking to Nathan. Kiki had to be looking for me by now. I had a job to do.

"Sorry. I'd love to, but I'm supposed to be networking right now." I gestured toward the crowd around us. "Talking to investors, trying to get prominent companies to notice me. That sort of thing."

I expected him to be disappointed. Maybe even angry. What I didn't expect was for him to let out another of those sharp barking laughs that sent a shiver up my spine, which I couldn't decide if I enjoyed or not.

"Oh, but that's perfect," he grinned just enough for a few of his teeth to show. His canines were particularly prominent, and I had a brief mental image of the big bad wolf about to gobble up little red riding hood. "I am an investor. I've just purchased *Fantaisiste*. I figured it was better than trying to build up a brand from scratch, but while it's technically a functioning company, I'm in desperate need of some new artistic talent. That's why I'm here, to scope out a new designer to hire."

Like most people in the fashion world, I'd heard of *Fantaisiste* before. They were a newer brand that had seemed to be on track to one day rival *Prada* or *Louis Vuitton*, but a few years ago they'd run into some money troubles and struggled to bounce back.

This guy had bought it?

The whole company?

He said it so casually too, like we were

discussing the merits of buying a new car versus a used car.

Before I could respond, he grabbed my wrist and pulled me from the bench. Although the room was just as crowded as before, Nathan apparently had a magical ability to make people move out of his way through his sheer presence alone. The crowd seemed to just part around him even though he didn't say a word. With little effort, he brought me to a door that led out of the banquet hall.

Out of the corner of my eye, I thought I saw Kiki among the crowd for a brief moment. Guilt gnawed at my stomach. I shouldn't just abandon her without a word. She'd be furious. Yet, I didn't have the heart to pull my hand out of Nathan's strong grip and I left the room with him.

If what Nathan said was true and he really was looking to hire a designer, and I managed to land the job, then surely Kiki would forgive me.

Beyond the banquet hall, the rest of the museum was practically empty. Its halls looked empty without guests to marvel at its displays, and the minimal lighting created a strange assortment of shadows that made the place look uninviting overall.

Just as Nathan had promised, on the far side of the museum there was a small racetrack where people could test drive some of the rare and classic cars. He had talked about convincing the staff to open it for us like the idea had just occurred to him, but he must have spoken to the museum staff earlier because they were already prepared when we got there.

"Any particular one you want to try?" he asked, indicating the line of cars parked beside the track.

Looking at the selection, I didn't have to think long as a cherry red frame caught my eye. "The Aston Martin would be fun," I said. "But I don't know how to drive a manual."

Nathan was already heading toward the Aston Martin before I'd even finished my sentence. He held the passenger door open for me. "Don't worry. I do."

Once inside and buckled in, the staff handed us the keys. The interior of the car looked like... well, it looked like a car. In the end, most modern cars looked basically the same on the inside. However, the quality of the materials they were made from was vastly different. I could tell how expensive the car was just by the butter soft texture of its leather seats.

"Do you want to learn?" Nathan suddenly asked.

"What?"

"How to drive a stick shift car. Do you want to learn?"

"Oh, um..." I glanced down nervously at the third pedal on the floor by his feet. "I guess."

"Don't worry about the pedals," he said as he grabbed my hand. "I can't really show you that from here. Let's just start with the different gears."

He placed my hand on the gear shifter, then pressed his own hand overtop of mine so we were both holding onto the stick.

"To get started, we need to first put it in neutral."

Squeezing my hand, he guided me to move the stick into the proper position. Then he turned the ignition, so the engine started rumbling.

"Then, to get going, you need to shift it into first gear."

Again, he squeezed my hand against the stick and moved it into the right position. With a few presses of the pedals on the floor, the car started moving, yet I didn't even glance out of the window, too distracted by the sight and feel of his hand controlling mine.

This pattern continued every time the car needed to switch gears, but even when the stick shifter wasn't needed, he still kept my hand trapped in place.

After one slower lap around the track, we started going faster until we were flying around each corner. Centripetal force pressed me back against my seat, like a hundred hands were pinning me down, and the car's engine purred gently beneath me.

We took the next turn faster than any before, and Nathan squeezed my hand against the stick tight enough that the leather handle ground into my palm.

I gasped. Hands weren't supposed to be an erogenous zone, but something about the heat and strength of his grip trapping my hand in place lit up every nerve in my body. Neither of us said a word as the atmosphere grew heavy between us. The lighting in the car was dim, shrouding everything in half shadow. Most of Nathan's expression was hidden as he watched the track, never once looking at me, but there was a spark in his expression that let me know he was acutely aware of the effect he was having on me.

We took the next turn just as fast, and he squeezed my hand again. I nearly moaned as I squirmed in my seat. Somehow, it would have been less intimate if he'd just put my hand on his dick. This oddly sensual yet innocent touch was driving me up the wall in a way I didn't know was possible.

CHAPTER THREE

Deacon

I never looked at my watch, so I had no idea how long we stayed in that car. By the end of it, as Nathan pulled the car back into its parking spot, I was biting my lip to keep myself under control. I was not going to be a cliché blushing virgin who came just from having their hand held. I wasn't even a virgin. Sure, I'd never gone quite... *that* far, but I'd certainly done enough other things that the title of virgin no longer applied to me.

The car came to a stop, and I tried desperately to calm my racing heart.

"Give me your phone."

I stared at Nathan dumbly for a moment, not comprehending the sudden demand.

He raised an eyebrow at me and smirked. "Your phone," he repeated, looking far too smug.

My hand was released from the stick shift for the first time since we started driving, and my fingers tingled as I pulled out my phone and handed it to him.

He quickly typed something into the device before handing it back to me. "My office. Ten o'clock on Monday. You're local, right?"

My brain still felt like it had been replaced with Jello and I struggled to keep up with what he was saying. "Um... yeah, I live nearby. It's why I was chosen when the designer who originally had my place in the show dropped out. I could get something together quickly."

"Good," Nathan nodded as he opened the door and stepped out of the car. "That'll make things easier."

I nodded for a moment as well, until I realized I had no idea what he meant. "Wait... what'll be easier?"

He leaned back into the open door, one arm braced against the car's frame. "To hire you as my new designer. Assuming you pass the interview, of course, but..." His gaze flickered up and down over me. "I don't think that'll be a problem for you."

Then he was gone, and I was left sitting alone in the car. I continued to sit there, dumbfounded, until the museum staff reminded me that they needed to put the car away.

Still half lost in a daze, I returned to the banquet, but I'd barely stepped through the door when I was immediately dragged out again.

"Where have you been," Kiki hissed under her breath as she pulled me toward the prep area that acted as the backstage for the runway. There were still people here as well, mostly other designers and models, but it was at least more private than the banquet room. "I have been looking everywhere for you. Did you get drunk? What..."

She trailed off as she got a good look at me. I knew how I must look. Rumpled and dazed, it probably seemed like I'd been up to something scandalous.

Her whisper turned into a screech as she started hitting my arm repeatedly. "Tell me you did not throw away everything we've been working for just to get laid."

"I didn't. I didn't. I… um, I think I got a job interview."

She finally stopped hitting me, but she still didn't look pleased. "A job interview? Where?"

"With *Fantaisiste*."

I thought she would be happy, but she just looked more upset. Or maybe that was disbelief twisting her face. "*Fantaisiste*? Really? Whose dick did you have to suck to get that?"

Suddenly feeling exhausted, I collapsed into one of the folding chairs set up backstage and rubbed at my temples. "I didn't do that. You know I'd never… sell myself like that. I just… spent some time talking with Nathan Sterling."

"Nathan Sterling?"

Kiki's tone caught my attention. She knew everything about every prominent figure in the high fashion world. I expected her to already know everything she needed to know just from a single name.

Instead, she started laughing so hard she doubled over.

"Deke. I love you, but you're an idiot.

I've researched everyone here and I've never even heard the name Nathan Sterling. You've been duped."

I just stared at her as she continued to laugh.

Had I been tricked?

To what end?

If Nathan and I had actually slept together, I might understand. Being lied to just to get me into bed would suck, but it was realistic.

Tricking me just to hold my hand didn't make sense.

As I sat there swimming in a mix of confusion and disbelief, a noise caught my attention. At first, I thought Kiki was still laughing oddly, but no, the sound was too far away.

Was someone else laughing?

It didn't sound right.

Curious, and a little worried, I stood up and wandered in the direction of the noise. Kiki called my name in question, but I didn't respond, so she ran after me.

Getting closer to the sound, I realized it wasn't laughter at all. Someone was screaming.

In the far corner of the backstage area, someone had opened a closet to reveal what looked like a large bundle of cloth.

A very familiar bundle of cloth.

Pushing aside the screaming person, I got a better look inside the closet.

It was the model who was supposed to present my original finale. She was wearing my missing dress, and she was very, very, dead.

CHAPTER FOUR

Nathan

Sitting in a police interrogation room was not how I envisioned my Saturday night. It wasn't the first time I'd been in such a situation, and certainly wouldn't be the last, but it still wasn't part of my plan for this weekend.

Or ever, really. Being subjected to a police investigation was almost never a part of my plans.

I'd had a reservation at Toca Madera for dinner tonight, which I was going to miss. Having to cancel that reservation put me on edge, and being forced to wait in the small cold room didn't help. When the police finally decided to show themselves and start their interrogation, they had better have a good reason for detaining me, or I'd be soothing my irritation in blood.

My night had been going so well, too. The fashion show had ended up being much more entertaining than I thought, and then I'd met Deacon, the designer with an interesting creative spark, and adorable dimples. His unique combination of cute with a rugged edge—hands calloused from working at a drawing table, but skin sun-kissed from spending time outside—was hard to ignore.

At first, I hadn't thought I'd find anyone who matched my taste. The fashion industry, while lucrative, was like a foreign world to me. So many people seemed determined to wear their uniqueness on their sleeve, everyone trying to outdo each other for who could stand out the most. I'd always preferred understated to overstated, and the clash of so many garish personalities was off-putting. I'd also never liked particularly effeminate men. Nothing wrong with them, but they did nothing for me.

I'd resigned myself to a night of business only, until I'd seen Deacon step onto the stage, taking a bow as he showed off his work. His light brown hair, artfully tousled, had gleamed with blond and copper highlights under the stage lights. The double-breasted vest he wore had shown off his narrow waist and lean muscular shoulders. His overall look, soft but with a masculine edge, had made me immediately want to get my hands on him.

Then, I'd spoken to him and found him actually interesting. He was a bit nervous when it came to polite conversation, but once I got him talking about something he cared about, his confidence and creativity shone in bright colors.

And he'd responded to me so beautifully, reacting with such sensitivity to the barest attention from me. I could have so much fun with him, both for business and pleasure, but instead of planning how to properly reel the man in, I was sitting in a police interrogation room.

If someone didn't come to speak with me in the next two minutes, I would walk out of the building. I was trying to be accommodating, but they couldn't keep me there without arresting me, and I hadn't done anything for them to arrest me.

Well, nothing that the police would know about.

Finally, the door opened, but instead of the local police, I was greeted by a face I unfortunately recognized.

"Agent Belden," I said, not bothering to pretend I didn't recognize the woman. "A pleasant surprise. I wasn't expecting to see you on this side of the Atlantic."

The woman just glared at me and took a seat at the table across from me. "Sterling. I wouldn't be in this country if not for you, so cut the crap and tell me what you're up to so I can go home."

Agent Lisa Belden was a member of Interpol. I'd run into her in England once when she was working on a case that ended up interfering with my business. Of course, nothing could be connected to me, but she'd been determined to catch me on something ever since.

"Eloquent as always, Agent. What exactly am I doing here?"

She started tapping a file against the desk without opening it, probably just to annoy me. "A woman was murdered at an event you attended."

I nodded and tried to ignore the tapping of the file. "Yes, and I've given my statement to the local police. I never even saw the poor girl until her body turned up, so I don't know what any of this has to do with me." The tapping of the file finally stopped, allowing silence to descend over the room once again. "For that matter, I don't know what this has to do with you. The murder of a fashion model isn't the jurisdiction of Interpol."

Agent Belden stood so she was looking down at me. It was probably an attempt to intimidate me, but I'd faced down much greater threats without flinching. Her act of aggression had the same threat level of a villain in a children's play.

"Anything involving you, Sterling, is the jurisdiction of Interpol. You caught our suspicion when you suddenly bought a fashion brand like *Fantaisiste,* and the first fashion event you attend, someone ends up dead. That isn't a coincidence."

Adjusting the cuffs of my suit, I stared up at her with a calm gaze that I knew must infuriate her. "You think I bought an entire high end fashion brand just to kill a model?"

I was definitely getting under her skin. An angry flush turned her cheeks patchy red and white, but to her credit she didn't lash out as much as she clearly wanted to. A single slam of her hand against the table was the only aggressive act she allowed herself before regaining her composure. "I don't know what your goal is yet, but whatever your organization has planned, I won't let you get away with it."

Just to infuriate her a wee bit more, I let myself smile a little wider, so my teeth flashed for a moment. To an outsider, it would look like a pleasant expression, but we both knew it was a threat. "Organization? I don't know what you're talking about. I'm just a businessman trying to get my foot into a new industry."

Realizing that her attempts at intimidation weren't working, Agent Belden stepped around the table to try and loom over my chair. Unfortunately, my height meant that even with her standing and me sitting, she wasn't that much taller than me.

One of her hands drifted toward the gun at her hip, though she didn't actually touch the weapon.

"Tell Zaur Dalkhan that he's made a mistake. That model you killed is the niece of the new FBI director. They aren't going to let this go so easily."

The FBI director?

Is that what this was about?

I'd heard recently that the director of the FBI had been killed in the line of duty—something about a pedophile ring, if I recalled correctly—and a new director had been instated.

For once, I could honestly say it had nothing to do with me. I didn't even need to lie as I stared Agent Belden directly in the eye. "I didn't kill anyone, and I don't know who you're talking about."

Well, the first part wasn't a lie, anyway. The second part of my statement was a lie, but even the cruelest torture wouldn't get me to admit that truth.

Zaur Dalkhan was, according to most international law enforcement, the leader of the Chechen Mafia. What they didn't know was that he was merely a figurehead leader. A red herring for them to chase blindly after.

He was also my half-brother. While he sat publicly on the throne as the head of the organization, I stood just behind him in the shadows, truly calling the shots. I'd changed my name, and westernized myself as much as possible so I could travel around without notice. Most people didn't even know I was originally from Chechnya. The few people who did know the truth about me, knew me only as The Wolf.

In this way, I could move freely, and lead our organization from the safety of the shadows.

Sitting in the harsh spotlights of the interrogation room, I stared up at Agent Belden without fear. She had nothing on me, and we both knew it. Based on our previous run-ins, she suspected that I had some tie to the Chechen Mafia. I'd kept an eye on her case against me when I realized she wouldn't give up her investigation. So far, she only suspected that I was an informant for the Chechen Mafia, or maybe an enforcer of some kind, and even that theory was based mostly off of guesswork. She had no proof I had any ties to the Chechen Mafia whatsoever, let alone my true place within the organization.

And she would never know. Even now, I could already see the look of defeat creeping into her eyes. She had nothing. There was nothing she could do to keep me from walking out the door.

Standing from my chair to stare down at her in turn, my smile grew a little wider. "I think we're done here. Thank you for a... pleasant evening, Agent Belden."

CHAPTER FIVE

Nathan

The police interrogation lasted several hours, going round and round as I continued to not give them the answers they were looking for. Eventually, they were forced to let me go since they had no evidence and I hadn't done anything wrong. Considering I hadn't been the one to kill the model, that outcome wasn't surprising. I was only annoyed that it took so long.

Agent Belden was especially livid as she watched me walk out the doors. I half expected her to pull her gun on me.

If she continued causing problems for

me, I really was going to have to take care of her, along with whoever had killed the model at the fashion show. Whether it was a sudden act of passion, or premeditated murder, the killer's actions were getting in my way, and had already brought law enforcement down on me.

As soon as I was free from the police station, I ordered my people to start their own investigation into the model's murder. The police were never going to catch the killer while Interpol kept them distracted looking at me. If I wanted it done right, I'd have to do it myself.

That brought me to Monday, and my anticipated interview with Deacon. It was a formality, really. I'd already decided to hire him. However, I could already tell he was a man who valued his work, and he wouldn't appreciate having a job just handed to him. He would want to feel like he earned it. Conducting an actual interview, a challenge he would have to surpass, would help with that.

Plus, I wasn't going to turn down the opportunity to play with him some more.

Since Las Vegas was one of my common stomping grounds, I had a permanent office in the city, but this wasn't mafia business. At least, it wasn't directly mafia business. Deacon's role as *Fantaisiste's* fashion designer would require nothing illegal. So, instead of my own personal office, I met him in *Fantaisiste's* corporate office I'd set up in the city.

It was still fairly new, but it was staffed by my own people, all of which I knew and had vetted personally, from the security guards down to the secretary outside my office door. So, it didn't surprise me that, although Deacon showed up on time for a meeting, it took nearly half an hour for him to actually make it through my staff and be allowed entry into my office.

I spent the time staring out the window, contemplating my new angle on a familiar city. The building was far enough away from the Vegas strip that I wasn't overshadowed by the massive casinos and resorts, but close enough that their neon lights still reached me. I always preferred to be just off to the side, hidden in the shadows where people wouldn't easily notice me.

So why did people keep trying to drag me into the light?

As I stared into the distance, I

wondered what to do about the Interpol agent breathing down my neck.

For her to have shown up so quickly at the merest hint of a crime happening in my vicinity, she must have already been close by. It felt like I was being hunted and I didn't like it. The coincidence of a model, who was actually the FBI director's niece, dying at a fashion show I just so happened to attend, rubbed all my instincts in all the wrong ways.

Finally, there was a knock on my door and Deacon was allowed inside my office. Just beyond the doorway, I noticed a blonde woman peering inside like she wanted to follow him, but then she was cut off by the heavy door closing. Deacon didn't seem to notice, but I knew that the door had locked behind him. It was just the two of us, alone in a soundproofed office, until I decided to open the lock.

"You know," Deacon said with a smile as he approached my desk. "My assistant thought that you were fake and just lying to me. Her face when we got here, and it turned out to be a real office, was priceless. So, either this is the most elaborate hoax ever arranged, or she was wrong for once. I'm not sure which is more unlikely."

Leaning back in my chair behind my desk, I stared up at him over my laced fingers. "Not a hoax. Please, sit."

Holding a leather folder to his chest, which probably held images and samples of his work, Deacon looked around for a chair on his side of the desk but found none. He didn't say anything but looked at me in confusion.

With a slight grin, I tapped the chair beside my own, which had gone overlooked.

An attractive blush spread over his cheeks, but he straightened his shoulders and came around to my side of the desk to sit beside me. "Here. I brought my portfolio. This Saturday's fashion show had a very specific theme, so it wasn't the best example of my overall work. My portfolio has a better general sampling, unless there's something specific you're looking for."

I flipped through a few pages in the portfolio, mostly out of courtesy. I'd already seen his work on the runway and didn't need any more proof of his skills.

"There is something specific I'm interested in."

Pulling out a magazine from the drawer of my desk, I tossed it down on the desk. The front cover advertised the new spring collection of clothing from a brand called *Minestra.*

Deacon looked at me in confusion. "*Minestra?* Yeah, they're not that old, but they've been making it big recently. What about them?"

"Just as a test, I want you to redesign a few of their outfits. Make something better that can compete with them in their own game."

Although Deacon still looked confused, he was automatically pulling out a sketchbook and pencils stored in the back of the portfolio case.

"Like, right now? I mean, sure. I can sketch something out real quick, but it won't be particularly good quality."

"It doesn't need to be," I said, flipping open the magazine to the spread page in the middle that showed the most of *Minestra's* new designs. "This is just a proof of concept, that your designs and abilities match what I need."

His pencil was already tapping on the paper, eager to draw, but he hesitated. "All right, I can do this, but... first, I need to know why? You're not up to something sketchy, are you?"

Yes, I was up to lots of things, but in this case I could actually answer honestly.

Well, mostly honestly.

Honesty was a novel concept in my life, and when presented with an opportunity for it, I jumped at the chance.

Placing my arm over the back of his chair, I leaned a little closer.

"A... colleague of mine did me a big favor a few years ago. I owe him. Now, the owner of this company..." I jabbed at the name *Minestra* written in metallic font across the glossy magazine page. "Is threatening him and he's asked for my help. I bought *Fantaisiste* so I could compete in the same industry and..." Leaning in even closer so I was almost speaking directly into Deacon's ear, I let my voice drop down into a pleasantly rough tone. "...take the bitch down a peg."

As I'd hoped, Deacon visibly shivered. He was dressed a little more casually than the outfit he'd worn at the fashion show. The sleeves of his shirt were rolled up to his elbows, and I watched as goosebumps broke out over the skin of his arms.

I fought the urge to run my hand over his skin and soothe him like one would a frightened animal, leaning back in my chair to remove myself from the temptation.

Still, nothing could tear my eyes away as I watched the bob of the Adam's apple in Deacon's throat as he swallowed. The man managed to regain his composure quickly, and pulled the magazine closer just to give his hands something to do.

"Must have been a big favor, if you're willing to buy a whole company and go to all this effort just to pay him back."

I couldn't help but laugh, though I kept the sound soft in respect for Deacon's close proximity. I'd been told in the past that my laugh could be off-putting, even terrifying, up close.

"D'Angelo thrives on big favors. It's practically how he makes his living. But yes, I owe him a lot, so I'm willing to do anything to protect him from someone threatening him. Plus, I was already toying with the idea of getting into the fashion industry, so if I can also make a profitable business at the same time, then it's a win-win. To do that, however, I need a designer capable of outshining

Minestra's own designs. I think you could be that designer, but I'll need to see the proof for myself before moving forward."

Seemingly coming to a decision, Deacon nodded to himself and started sketching out some ideas. As he'd said, the drawings were quick and rough, just a suggestion of an idea rather than a polished presentation, but that was all I needed for now.

It took some time. Even the most proficient artists couldn't pull something out of thin air. His pencil flew over the page, bringing recognizable forms to life with just a few lines. He even seemed to have his own style of shorthand symbols marking fabric types and other design elements that couldn't be shown in black and white. It was a fascinating process, but I didn't want to crowd him, so I tried not to stare too much.

With time to myself to think, I remembered a detail about the model's death at the fashion show that I'd forgotten. Deacon had been the one to report the body, and apparently the victim had been wearing his missing dress.

"Did the police give you a hard time?"

"Hmm?" He made a vaguely

questioning sound without looking up from the page he was working on.

"You found the body, and apparently, she was wearing your dress. I imagine the police had a lot of questions for you."

Even when he looked up from the page, his fingers never actually stopped moving. He seemed to read the page like Braille, and continued to bring his vision to life.

"Surprisingly, no. I thought I was going to be in the police station all weekend answering questions, but after taking my statement and hearing my summary of what happened, they dismissed me. I haven't heard back from them since."

That was concerning. Even if Deacon wasn't a suspect in the model's death, the fact that she had been intended to present Deacon's work meant that he should at least be a person of interest.

It seemed my instinct to investigate the case on my own had been right. So long as Agent Belden was focused on me, no one was going to look into anything else.

As these thoughts ran through my mind, Deacon had already returned to his sketchbook.

"It must have been shocking," I said,

keeping my voice gentle in case I was touching on a sensitive topic. "Finding a dead body like that."

To my surprise, he just shrugged. "I didn't actually find it, but the person who did find it was too busy screaming to actually do anything useful, so I reported it." Placing his pencil down, he slid his sketchbook over to me. "Although, it certainly wasn't how I pictured ending my night. Now, here, take a look at these designs. Do these match what you're thinking of? Remember, these are just off the top of my head, so they aren't final or anything."

He seemed more nervous presenting me his designs than he did talking about the dead body he'd literally found two days ago. I was intrigued, but this wasn't the right situation for me to pry. Instead, I simply picked up the sketchbook and flipped through the designs.

When sketching out an idea, many designers drew blank models standing in generic T-poses that exposed every element of the design. Deacon, however, drew his models in some sort of motion to show off how the garment would move with them. His drawings felt more alive than many of the actual outfits I'd seen on the runway at the fashion show.

"Perfect," I praised him. "This is just what I'm looking for." Smiling, I handed him back the sketchbook along with his portfolio. "Assuming the hiring paperwork all checks out, by the end of the week you can call yourself a member of my team."

"Great," Deacon said, though he had an odd look on his face. He stood up, looking down at me in an oddly similar pose to the way Agent Belden had tried to intimidate me, but there was nothing aggressive in his posture. "Now that we've got that settled, answer me this. Are you hitting on me?"

After everything I'd experienced in my forty-six years of life, I didn't think I could be shocked by anything, but apparently, I was wrong. No one had ever asked me such a question so bluntly before, and I didn't know what to say in response.

"I... would hope the answer to that question was obvious. I've not been subtle."

Deacon nodded, agreeing with me, though the gesture seemed to be more for his sake than mine. "Yeah, I thought so. I just... wasn't sure if you were being serious or not."

Standing, so I no longer had to look up at him, I let my hands hang loosely at my sides to avoid reaching out to him or making any sort of accidentally aggressive move. "And if I was being serious? How would you feel about that?"

His mouth scrunched to one side as he thought, emphasizing the dimples on his cheeks. The slight beard on his face seemed like it was meant to hide those dimples, but they were too prominent to be ignored.

I also wouldn't call his facial hair a beard. At most, I would call it nicely groomed stubble. Back in my home country, men traditionally wore robust beards several inches long at the minimum. When I'd shaved my own beard in order to fit in better with the western world, my face had felt cold for days. By comparison, Deacon was practically clean-shaven, though I knew that probably wasn't what he was going for. His "beard" was likely meant to add strength to his face and keep him from looking too cute.

It was a useless attempt, especially when he made such endearing expressions that just made me want to pin him down and kiss him.

At such close proximity, when he finally looked up and met my gaze, I noticed the abundance of green and amber radiating out from the center of his hazel eyes, like the rays of a spring sun.

"If you are serious, then you need to be upfront," he declared. "I don't like playing games or beating around the bush. If you are interested in me that way, then... do something about it."

I thought I was shocked a moment ago, but once again I was wrong. That was just surprise. What I felt now was true shock.

I'd been given an invitation I couldn't refuse.

Quickly stepping forward, I backed him up until he pressed against the desk. Placing my hands on the desktop on either side of him, caging him in, I slipped my leg between his so our hips ground together.

"Mark your words," I whispered directly into his ear. "I'm not a patient man. Once you invite me in, I won't hesitate to take what I want."

I watched the thoughts bounce around

behind his eyes as he debated with himself, but after a moment, he grabbed the lapels of my suit and pulled me closer.

That was it. He was mine, and I wasn't letting him go.

CHAPTER SIX

Deacon

Nathan kissed like a typhoon. Intense, powerful, and impossible to stop once started. All I could do was cling to his shoulders and try to hold on for the ride. Even kissing him back, sealing my mouth over his and tangling his tongue with my own, made me feel like a puppet being led through a dance rather than an equal participant.

Before I realized what was happening, I lost my balance and fully sat on the desk. My feet were off the floor, and only my grip on his shoulders kept me upright.

When we finally parted, I was panting

like I'd just run from one end of the desert to the other, overwhelmed yet still parched.

"This… is this how you always interview potential employees?"

He leaned forward so I could feel his erection grinding against mine.

"The interview started and ended the moment you stepped through that door. All you had to do was show up." He pulled back just enough to put an inch of air between us, and I instinctively gripped him tighter. "If all you're looking for is a job, then it's yours. You can walk out of here right now and start working. No questions asked. However… if you're interested in more…" He nipped at my bottom lip with his teeth, startling a gasp out of me. "I can offer that, too."

I should have said "no". All I wanted was a job to further my career, and now I had it. Nathan's offer to be the lead designer for a major fashion company was more than I'd been hoping for. Yet, now that I had achieved my goal, something greedy and insatiable welled up inside me.

I wanted more than just a career. I wanted thrill, and Nathan Sterling was nothing if not thrilling.

Wrapping one of my legs around his hips, I pulled him closer and chased away the space he'd put between us.

"More. Definitely more."

He sighed in relief, kissing me again so passionately that I fell flat against the desk. Something tumbled off the desk and crashed to the floor, but I didn't care enough to look. If Nathan was worried about the contents of his desk, he didn't show it. He didn't even seem to be aware that we'd knocked something over as his hands started wandering down my body.

"Good," he gasped when the kiss ended. "I said you could walk out of here no questions asked, but I might have been lying. I'm not sure I could have let you go so easily."

Was he joking or should I take that threat seriously?

More importantly, did I care?

I probably should. I'd had bad experiences with people being too forceful in the past. Memories of my second, and last, boyfriend came to mind.

I shuddered.

Yet, I didn't get the same feeling from Nathan. Although the man claimed he wouldn't let me go, the way he held me said differently. His hands felt like a cradle rather than a shackle. I could leave their grip if I wanted, but why would I want to when it was so much more comfortable to stay exactly where I was.

Rather than try to explain all that, however, I just ran a hand through his hair and pressed a series of kisses down his neck. He was fully clothed, so I still couldn't see the tattoos hidden beneath, but I caught a glimpse of something that looked like a snake on his neck.

How far did the tattoos go?

There were also some signs of ink peeking out of the cuffs of his sleeves.

Were these the only ones, or was there a whole canvas of artwork hidden beneath his clothing?

Within his dark hair, there was some gray at his temples. He was obviously older than me, but I was hardly a fresh-faced teenager myself. Twenty-eight may not seem old to a lot of people, it probably didn't even seem old to Nathan, but it was enough for me to know what I wanted and what I didn't want.

I wanted him, consequences be damned.

KISSING DANGER

One of his hands crept under my shirt while the other started to undo the clasp of my pants. I didn't have the confidence to do the same to him, but I did dare to slip a hand into his back pocket. Even through the thick material of his pants, I could feel the firmness of his muscular physique. Every inch of the man seemed to have been carved from rock. A real-life walking statue, come to life specifically for the purpose of ravaging me.

I sucked at the skin of his neck, determined to leave a mark. This might be our only time together. We hadn't discussed what this encounter actually meant. Even if we never interacted as more than professionals after this, he was going to walk out of here with evidence of me carved into his flesh.

The moment my teeth touched his skin, his breathing turned erratic. I wasn't surprised that Nathan liked things a little rougher. He seemed like the type to prefer a dominant role in bed. However, I was surprised by how quickly he responded. Surely, he had plenty of experience. The slight sting of an aggressive hicky shouldn't be enough to get him excited.

There wasn't time for me to ponder this discovery further. By then, he'd succeeded in undoing my pants, pulling them down a few inches so my waist and hips were exposed. The feeling of my mouth at his neck seemed to have spurred him into action, and he pushed his hand deeper into my pants to squeeze my ass in a demanding grip.

Before I even realized what was happening, one of my legs lashed out and kicked him in the hip. He grunted and stumbled back a step, nearly tripping over the office chair behind him.

I stared at him from my position sprawled over the desk, shocked and bewildered over my own actions. He was also obviously confused, looking between me and himself like he didn't understand what just happened.

Realizing what I'd done, my shock turned to shame. In a panic, I started apologizing so quickly my words all slurred together.

"I'm so sorry. I didn't mean... I shouldn't have... That wasn't what I meant. I don't know why I did that."

That last part was a lie. I knew exactly why I'd reacted that way. I just thought I was over it by now. So stupid. I was a grown man, nearly thirty years old. Sex shouldn't be this hard or nerve-wracking.

I didn't realize I'd been mumbling to myself the whole time until Nathan tipped my head up by the chin and forced me to look at him.

"Have I overstepped? You seem... uncomfortable."

"No, it's not... I definitely want this. I just..."

What was I supposed to say?

The explanation felt so childish. However, the only other option was to let Nathan think he'd done something wrong, and that was unacceptable.

Still sitting on the desk, I curled one leg up against my chest and wrapped my arms around my knee like I was hugging a childhood toy. It probably made me look younger than I was, but at that moment I didn't care.

"I've never... The idea of having someone... inside me, has always kinda freaked me out. I don't know why. It's just always made me nervous."

I could see the thought in his eyes the moment it flickered though his mind and I quickly waved my hands to dispel it away.

"I'm not a virgin. I've done plenty of stuff, just... not that."

The troubled look still didn't leave his eyes, and with a quiet sigh, he pulled the desk chair closer to sit down. The position put him lower than me, so I had to look down at him. My legs fell to either side of the chair as I faced him, and he placed his hands tentatively on my knees as if testing to see if his touch was still acceptable.

"I'm sorry," I said, and set my hands over his to keep them there, letting him know that his touch was very much wanted. "I'm ruining the mood, aren't I?"

"Not ruining anything," he said as his thumbs traced the seams of my pants along my inner thigh. "However, don't lie to me."

I immediately tried to protest, to assure him that I wasn't lying. One look from his hazel eyes, as sharp as a diamond blade, silenced me.

"Being nervous about penetrative intercourse is fine."

Something about the clinical way he said "penetrative intercourse" made me blush in embarrassment. If felt like he was a teacher giving me my first Sex-Ed lesson.

"However," he continued, adding extra emphasis to his words to make sure I was listening. "That wasn't a nervous reaction. You literally struck me to get me away from you. That is the reaction of someone who is genuinely afraid, and you didn't even seem to realize you were doing it. That is more than just natural nervousness over something you haven't done before."

Everything he said was a statement, yet a question was woven through his words. He wanted answers about my reaction, but he wasn't going to ask outright. It was my decision whether or not to tell him.

Taking a deep breath, I started what I knew would be an awkward explanation.

"I said it used to be fine, and that's the truth. My first boyfriend, when I was in high school, hated how reluctant I was about sex. I tried to keep him happy with other things, but it was never enough, and we eventually broke up. It was sad, but fine. Later, when I was in college, I tried dating again, but the nervousness was still there, even worse than before.

Again, I tried to compensate in other ways, and I enjoyed everything we did, but it was never enough. We'd only been dating for about two weeks when he... got more insistent."

Nathan's grip on my legs tightened until I could feel the stitching of my own pants. "Did he force you?"

"No," I was quick to reassure him. "I didn't let it get that far."

Instead of looking reassured, as I'd hoped, Nathan just looked more upset.

"That fact that you had to stop it from going so far means that being forced was a possibility. Even if it didn't happen, your own lover was willing to go that far and force you into something you didn't want."

"Yeah, well..." I shrugged, not sure what to say. "I left before it got that bad, and obviously broke up with him. Haven't seen the bastard since. It's fine."

I was trying to have a serious conversation, but Nathan's hands had started stroking up and down my legs. It was probably meant as a soothing gesture, but I just found it distracting, like I was being teased with something I couldn't have.

"*Fine* is not the word I would use," Nathan said with a frown, seemingly oblivious to the effect his hands were having on me. "If you're still reacting so aggressively to just being touched, even years later..."

I immediately cut him off. "No. It's not affecting me. I mean, yeah, it did for a while. For, like, a year after I broke up with my second boyfriend I would freak out and push people away whenever they got too handsy, but I got over it. I just... wasn't paying attention this time. It's been a while since I was intimate with anyone. Too busy with my career, you know. So, I forgot to control my reaction. Sorry. It won't happen again. I promise."

Standing up so he was once again leaning over me, Nathan planted his hands on the desk on either side of my hips. "You shouldn't have to control your reactions in order to enjoy sex. Now, if you're still interested in pursuing something with me—"

"Yes," I cut him off, nodding eagerly as I once again gripped the lapel of his jacket to pull him closer.

Nathan let out a single barking laugh with enough force to ruffle my hair. "I'm glad you're so enthusiastic, but please listen to my whole proposition before agreeing." One of his hands left the desk to cup my face and stroke my cheek. "If you're still interested in pursuing something with me, then how about we start slow and work our way up. See if we can get you comfortable with everything sex has to offer."

Maybe it was due to the fact that arousal was clouding my brain, but I didn't need to think about his proposition very long before agreeing.

"That sounds great, but..." I hesitated for a moment as reality cut through the hormones turning my brain to soup. "But what if I can't? What if I'm never comfortable enough to give you what you want?"

Our foreheads pressed together in an oddly intimate gesture, so close that our breath mingled.

"You're already giving me what I want just by being here," Nathan said softly. "However, if you mean what will happen if you're never comfortable enough to really let me fuck you... Well, like you said before, there's plenty of other things we can do."

The sound of such a crude word coming from his lips lit a spark of arousal in me, and I let my hands travel down his torso to fumble for his belt buckle.

"Oh, yes. That I can do."

Before I'd even gotten the buckle undone, he stopped me.

"Not like that. I have a feeling you've always been the one putting in more effort. We're going to do things a little differently."

I looked up at him confused, but he merely gave me a wicked grin in return.

"Lie back."

His hand on my chest pushed me backward until I was lying flat on the desk again. For a moment, my nerves returned as he stood between my legs and slid my pants down until they were all the way off my hips.

"Wait, what are you—"

Before I could finish the question, he shocked me into silence by dropping to his knees in front of the desk.

He pulled my legs over his shoulders and pinned my hips to the desk. His mouth found my cock and he started sucking me eagerly.

"Wha— Oh god. You're..." I tangled my

hands in his hair, feeling the motion of his head without pushing him away or pulling him closer. I wasn't even sure what to do other than let him have his way with me.

It was true, since I could never go as far as my partners wanted, I always ended up on my knees, offering my mouth as compensation. I couldn't remember the last time someone had done such a thing for me.

Although I had little experience on this side of a blowjob, I could tell one thing for certain. This wasn't Nathan's first time performing in such a way. His mouth moved with too much confidence, easily finding every sensitive spot on my cock with his tongue and taking me all the way to the back of his throat without gagging.

He'd done this before. An image of Nathan on his knees for previous lovers, pleasuring them with his mouth just like he was doing for me, sprung to mind, and jealousy sunk its bitter teeth into my heart.

I came after an embarrassingly short time. My orgasm snuck up on me quick and sharp. I barely had time to warn Nathan before the pleasure building in my gut snapped and I erupted in his mouth.

I still clung to his hair so tightly; I was surprised I didn't pull any out. I hoped Nathan's office was soundproofed; otherwise everyone in the building was going to know what we were doing from the sound of my shouting.

Only when I'd calmed down enough to breathe without panting, and removed my hands from his hair, did I realize that he'd kept me in his mouth the whole time. He'd swallowed my pleasure like a pro, and when he looked up at me with a glint in his eye, he licked his lips just to taunt me.

Oh, yeah.

Nathan definitely had plenty of experience. For the first time in years, I actually felt like a virgin in comparison.

He was also obviously aroused, his pants so tented I was surprised he hadn't popped the stitching of his fly.

"Come here." I beckoned him closer. "Let me take care of that."

I expected him to insist I get on my knees and return the favor, and I was more than happy to do so. However, instead of letting me off the desk, he kept me flat on my back and leaned over me until his face was buried against my neck. Opening his pants just enough to pull his erection free, he started stoking himself while sucking bruises into my skin.

I couldn't see exactly what he was doing, but the sounds and the suggestion of his motions caught my imagination better than if I'd been able to directly watch him. My blood was already turning hot, and while I couldn't get aroused again so quickly, I had no doubt that it would take very little effort.

Lying there without participating was torture. I couldn't sit still. With a hand in his hair, I raised his head off my neck and kissed him instead. He grunted in surprise, but quickly realized I didn't mind the taste of myself on his lips. To the contrary, the secretly possessive corners of my heart enjoyed tasting the evidence of what he'd just done for me, and I eagerly licked into his mouth.

The motion of his hand sped up, and it wasn't long before he was moaning into my mouth as he came as well. At some point while I wasn't looking, he'd grabbed a tissue off the box on the desk, so he didn't stain either of our clothes. I appreciated it, because I was fond of the shirt I was wearing—one of my own creations, of course—but I also wouldn't have minded walking out of the office wearing the obvious evidence of our shared pleasure.

We took a few moments to clean up using the office's meager supplies. Afterward, we were technically presentable, but there was also no denying what we'd just done. Nothing could hide the satisfied daze in my eyes, or the way his hair didn't quite lie flat again after having my hands tangled in it.

"So," Nathan said, leaning back casually in his office chair as if half the items usually placed on his desk weren't currently scattered over the floor. "I'll send you the details of the job. Can you get started by the end of the week?"

I couldn't help but laugh as I finished pulling my clothes back into place. "End of the week? Ha. I'll be planning out new ideas on the journey home. You're..." I gave him what I hoped was an alluring smile. "Quite the creative inspiration, Mister Sterling."

While my smile had been flirtatious, his returning grin was pure sin.

"Happy to lend a hand, Mister Millar."

CHAPTER SEVEN

Deacon

I was hanging in mid-air, fifty feet off the ground, when my phone started ringing. Making sure that my feet and my left hand all had secure purchase on the rocky cliff-face, I let go with my right hand to press the button on the Bluetooth speaker in my ear.

"Kiki. What's up?"

She didn't answer immediately, and I took a moment to find a new grip for my right hand on the cliff.

"I can hear you panting," she said, after a moment. "Which means you're either having sex, or rock climbing, and

I'm not sure which idea I hate more."

"What's wrong with rock climbing?" I whined, completely ignoring her comment about sex. She obviously knew what I'd done with Nathan on the day of my interview, and we had both silently agreed not to bring it up.

Through the phone, her voice took on a nagging edge, like a mother berating their wayward child. "Rock climbing is going to mess up your hands. You're an artist. Your career is defined by what you can make with your hands."

I laughed, while at the same moment spotting my next handhold a few feet up the cliff. It would be a stretch, but I should be able to reach the promising crack in the rock.

"You're acting like I'm some world-renowned concert violinist. I promise, after this, I will still be able to hold a pencil and work a sewing machine."

She huffed loud enough to be heard through the phone. "There's no point arguing with you. You never listen to me."

Pushing up with my legs, I reached for the next grip that I'd spotted, but it was farther away than I thought. Even stretching all my limbs to their full length,

I couldn't quite reach.

"Are you kidding? Half my time is spent doing whatever you say."

"Which means half your time is spent disobeying me. All my work won't matter when you end up undoing it all anyway."

No choice. I was going to have to jump for the next grip.

"So sorry, Master. Your humble servant will aim to do better."

Pushing off with my legs, I flew weightless through the air for a moment before my right hand found the grip in the rock I'd been aiming for. The full weight of my body strained against my shoulder, and I felt my muscles fighting against the pull of gravity, but my grip held strong, and I was able to find new purchase on the cliff for my feet.

"Please tell me you didn't just fall," Kiki's voice whispered through the speaker in my ear.

"All good. No falling. I've been rock climbing since I was a kid. I know what I'm doing."

"Hmmm." She obviously didn't want to argue, but I could tell just from the sound of her noncommittal noise that she was still questioning my overall sanity.

"Just finish up with your thrill-seeking and get yourself back to the studio. We still have work to do to get ready for this new job."

"As you command," I agreed. Twisting away from the cliff wall as much as I could, I cast my gaze over the beauty of the Nevada horizon. "I was going to finish up soon anyway. It's almost sunset."

Brilliant oranges and reds streaked through the sky, turning the landscape into a portrait of fire and rock. Nothing could beat the radiance of a desert sunset.

The quickly fading sun beat down on the back of my neck and sweat beaded along my hairline as I pulled myself over the top of the cliff. Heaving for breath, I lay on the ground and stared up at the sky, reveling in the deep-seated exhaustion that set into my muscles.

After my "interview" with Nathan, I'd been on edge for days. The man was an addiction. Now that my libido had been awakened, I couldn't get enough, but I didn't know when I would see him again. So, I was left strung-out and twitterpated, like ants running around under my skin, I couldn't sit still long enough to stitch two pieces of fabric together, let alone create an entire line of new outfits.

I needed to burn off the excess energy, and so I'd turned to my tried-and-true method. Rock climbing, or some similarly extreme outdoor activity, usually helped to settle my nerves when I was feeling on edge. This time was no exception. Already, as the sky darkened above me, I could feel my mind calming down. Like navigating a kayak down a river full of rapids and finally reaching the safety of calm waters, I could breathe normally again.

The sky had turned mostly purple by the time I finished storing away my climbing gear in the saddlebag of my motorcycle. It wasn't quite night yet, but the first eager stars were already making their appearance.

Putting my motorcycle helmet over sweaty hair wasn't a pleasant experience, but while I enjoyed thrill-seeking activities, I had no intention of actually risking my life. The helmet was absolutely required whenever I rode my bike, so I sucked it up and dealt with the unpleasant sensation of sweaty hair being crushed against my scalp.

The climbing area I'd chosen that day

was on the opposite side of the city from my studio, which meant I had to either drive all the way around the city, or dive straight through it. Spring in Las Vegas wasn't the busiest time for tourists, but the city could never be called quiet. Even during the off-season, the streets were packed with traffic and people were bustling about shoulder to shoulder.

Some locals hated the chaos that tourists brought, but I didn't mind. That constant thrum of life was the reason I'd moved to Las Vegas in the first place. Everywhere I looked, there were new possibilities for creative inspiration. The flashing neon lights of the casinos that lined the main street lit up the night sky like an artist's brush as I weaved my bike through the dense traffic.

Maybe I should try catching some of those colors in my new creations. Adding metallic or shimmery fabric would mean having to change some of the designs I'd already planned, but it would be worth it in the end. I wasn't afraid of a little more work if it meant creating the art exactly as I wanted.

Night had fully settled over the city when I finally pulled into the little parking lot outside my studio. It wasn't in the busiest part of the city, and you wouldn't even know it was a design studio just by looking at the outside, but it was mine. Every penny had been paid for by my own hard work.

Kiki met me at the front door. "Ugh. You're a mess."

I looked down at myself and grimaced. Not only was there obvious sweat soaking through my clothes, but the desert clay had left a film of fine red dust coating every inch of me.

"I'll shower before I even step foot in the studio. Don't worry."

Kiki sniffed, offended by the very idea of dirt, and clearly not understanding my need for strenuous outdoor activity.

"Whatever. Just hurry up. We've got a lot to get done in order to move to the new studio."

I was in the process of opening the door to the building when I froze with my key still in the lock.

"Wait. New studio?"

Heaving a heavy sigh, Kiki finished unlocking the door for me and pushed her way inside to escape the desert heat, which she detested.

"Yes. Did you actually read any of the information Sterling sent over to us about your new job? You'll be getting a studio within their building. For a job like this, you can't just be off designing things on your own. You have to be part of the whole production process."

"Oh. Right."

I'd known all that information, but it hadn't really registered to me what that meant. We were moving to a new studio.

Did that mean I would have to leave this one behind?

Sure, the new studio would probably be much larger and grander, but it wouldn't really feel like mine. It would just be a space that someone else gave me.

There wasn't time to process this as Kiki hustled me off to the studio's bathroom for a shower, making sure I didn't even look at the work area where half-finished outfits lay spread out over the tables and floors. I almost felt insulted.

Did she really believe I would risk getting dirt on any of the expensive fabric after all the effort I'd put in to select it?

Such a thing would practically be a

sacrilege to my designer's heart.

My shower was quick and thorough. Not the luxurious relaxation I would prefer, but needs won out over wants. If we were moving to a different studio, then there was a lot of work we really needed to get done.

I was still drying my hair when I stepped into the studio, naked except for a towel wrapped around my waist. My spare clothes were in a drawer on the other side of the room, and Kiki wouldn't care about the sight of my bare chest. She was as gay as I was, and nothing about the male physique interested her.

Being greeted by a woman's voice upon entering the room didn't surprise me. The fact that I didn't recognize the voice, however, did.

"Mister Deacon Millar," the woman standing in the middle of my studio said, with barely any inflection in her voice.

The towel I'd been using to dry my hair dropped from my hand, and I clutched the one around my waist to make sure it stayed in place. "Who the hell are you?"

"Agent Belden of Interpol." She flashed her badge so quickly I barely knew what I was looking at, not that I knew what an

Interpol badge was supposed to look like anyway. "I have a few questions for you."

"Fine, I'll answer yours if you answer mine. I'll go first. What the hell are you doing here?"

The agent came closer, her heeled boots creating a decisive sound against my floorboards with each step.

"You've got attitude. It's no wonder Sterling likes you."

I stepped back, accidentally kicking over a box sitting on the floor, and flinched as a roll of expensive cloth rolled across the room.

"What'd you mean? What does Nathan have to do with anything?"

The Agent pretended to look around my studio, but I could tell she was watching my every move. "Nathan? Hmm. From what I know, he doesn't let many people call him by his first name." She started searching through a box of spare bobbins and pins, taking her time like she had every right to be there. She was obviously trying to aggravate me on purpose, but I didn't have enough patience to avoid the trap even though I knew what she was doing.

"Hey, rewind for a moment. Why are

you talking about Nathan? Why are you even here?"

Agent Belden finally stopped messing around and faced me directly, and I had an uneasy feeling that I was little more than an interesting lab rat in her eyes.

"A woman was killed at an event you were a part of, wearing one of your dresses. It can't be a surprise that law enforcement would be looking into it."

Crossing my arms, it was easy to ignore the feeling of the air conditioner blowing over my bare damp skin. Less easy to ignore, however, was my instinct to desperately clutch the towel wrapped around my waist like I was a blushing maiden afraid for my virtue.

"I was already interviewed by the police. You said you're Interpol? What does a model's death have to do with international law enforcement?"

It was probably a bad idea to question the woman with a gun standing in the middle of my studio. This was usually where Kiki would step in to save me from my own impulsive stupidity.

Where was she, anyway?

The studio wasn't that big. She surely would have heard our conversation by now and come to investigate our guest.

My question seemed to have triggered something in the Agent, for her faux-casual tone dropped to reveal her true seriousness.

"What is your relationship with Nathan Sterling?"

Of all the things I expected her to ask about, that wasn't even on the list.

A blush heated my cheeks and spread down my neck to my chest. Mostly naked as I was, my reaction was unfortunately very obvious.

"That... isn't any of your business."

Agent Belden rolled her eyes, and for a moment I could imagine the teenager she used to be. "I'm not asking about your sex life." She shuddered, as if just thinking about it made her skin crawl. I wasn't sure if it was meant as an insult to me or Nathan, but the meaning was still loud and clear. "I mean, what business do you have with him? Nathan Sterling suddenly takes an interest in the fashion industry, and the first event he attends, a woman is murdered. The victim was one of your models, and then Sterling immediately offers you a job."

She spoke a lot of words, but there

was obviously even more being said between her sentences. Accusations were being made without ever being voiced.

Although I quickly managed to figure out what she was implying, it took several moments for me to respond because I couldn't believe what my own ears were telling me.

"You think I killed that model? For what? For a job? For Nathan? Why would he care about killing some random model?"

Agent Belden stalked toward me, forcing me to back up until I hit the drafting table in the middle of the room. It was a perverse mirror of my last interaction with Nathan, but far more terrifying and far less arousing.

"That model happened to be the FBI director's niece. I don't believe in coincidences. Sterling killed that girl, even if he didn't do it with his own hands. Getting other people to do his dirty work fits his MO. I've seen it before. So, for your sake, I hope whatever he offered you is worth a lifetime prison sentence, because that's what you're looking at when you're caught. And make no mistake. You will be caught."

Situations like this were exactly why I needed an assistant to manage me. I hated being challenged, and I especially hated being threatened. The two together triggered my impulsivity like nothing else could.

Gripping the towel around my waist to keep it firmly in place, I stood tall and used my slightly greater height to stare down at the Agent. "*Caught* isn't the word you're looking for. I can't be *caught* for something I didn't do. Maybe I can be *framed*, but I can't be *caught*. So, if you want to catch the killer, you need to look elsewhere."

Sighing deeply, Agent Belden backed off, looking around my studio again. "Pity. You're a good artist, but apparently, you're not very smart. I guarantee you'll be in handcuffs the next time I see you, assuming Sterling doesn't take care of you himself."

If this were a movie, I'd get the last word with a clever comeback as she was heading out the door. Unfortunately, all I could think of doing at that moment was to glare at the back of her head until she left. My pulse was pounding in my ears, and it took me several moments to calm down and regain enough sense to remember that Kiki was still missing.

After a few minutes of searching, I found Kiki locked in a backroom closet, furious as a hissing kitten, and on the verge of committing a murder of her own.

CHAPTER EIGHT

Nathan

Finding the person who killed the model at the fashion show was surprisingly easy. They were barely trying to hide, as if they wanted to be caught. The man was completely unremarkable, and I could tell as soon as I saw him that he was just a hired lackey, barely worth my time.

Still, I needed answers from him, and since Interpol had already gotten involved, I needed to be extra thorough and handle things myself.

In a small shack out in the middle of the desert, the non-descript man knelt at my feet, hands restrained behind his back, and one of his eyes missing from its socket. The empty hole where an eye had once been slowly oozed dark blood down the side of his face, which caused his lips to stick together as he begged.

"Please. I didn't know. I was just paid to kill the woman. I thought it was a jealous lover or something. I didn't know she was involved with you."

A drop of blood fell off his chin and nearly landed on my shoe. I pulled my foot away at the last moment to avoid the stain and kicked the man square in the chest to get him away from me. He fell on his back, sputtering as he choked on his own blood.

"That woman isn't involved with me. Now, stop babbling and tell me who hired you, what exactly you were hired for, and why."

With his hands tied, and disoriented from blood loss, the man couldn't right himself on his own. A pair of the guards I'd brought with me were forced to gather him off the floor and place him back on his knees right in front of my chair.

"I-I-I never saw the person who hired me. They never gave me a name. Anonymous messages and payment drop-offs only."

Using an old pipe I'd found in the shack, I tipped the man's head up to face me directly. "I know that, but surely they told you something."

I let the end of the rusty pipe hover just an inch from his remaining eye, needing no words to explain what I intended to do with it if he didn't tell me what I wanted to know.

The man was obviously a professional, who had probably claimed dozens, if not hundreds, of lives. Death wouldn't scare a man like this. Disability, however, was a different story. The threat of living with a broken body could crumble even the steeliest nerves.

Watching the man's resistance wither before my eyes, I nearly laughed. There were millions of people all over the world who lived their entire lives disabled in one way or another, and they managed just fine. Yet, to a man like this, whose ego and self-worth were tied explicitly to his physical capabilities, taking away something that plenty of people lived without was worse than a death sentence.

"There... there was one thing," he finally said, treating each word as if it was tearing out a piece of his soul on the way out of his mouth. "The person who hired me. Their last message had an extra note at the end. It said... It said, 'The hidden wolf has no pack, but the blossom on the tree shares many roots.' There was no explanation about what it meant."

The man trembled, afraid that I would be upset by his nonsensical answer. However, I merely smiled and lowered the pipe. Such a phrase may not make sense to him—it probably wouldn't even make sense to most outsiders—but I knew exactly what it meant.

The imagery of 'the hidden wolf' was easy. It obviously referred to me. Since my name wasn't well known, I was often simply referred to as 'The Wolf' due to my home country's symbolic animal.

Even the guards I'd brought with me today didn't know my status within the Chechen Mafia. They obviously knew I was someone important, but had no idea they were standing beside their leader.

'The blossom', however, would have been more difficult to figure out if it were not for one crucial piece of information I already knew.

Caprice Vidales, the head of the

Vidales family that D'Angelo had asked me to handle for him, was well known to most Mafia families. She'd put a lot of effort into spreading her name far and wide. However, most people didn't know that she had not been born under the Vidales name. She'd married into the family and immediately took over leadership as soon as her nuptials were finished. Before marriage, her name had been Caprice Fiore.

It was a small, almost powerless family whose surname meant "flower".

Caprice had left this little message with the assassin to taunt me. She knew I was targeting her as a favor to D'Angelo, yet she was certain that no matter what I did, I would never be able to overcome her.

Killing the model had been a setup just to get Interpol on my case as a way to scare me off.

Never mind my promise to D'Angelo. Caprice had sealed her fate with this one sentence. She had challenged me, even gloated in my face, and I couldn't abide such an act of disrespect.

Standing from my chair, I tossed the old pipe aside and wiped the rust stains from my hands.

"Thank you for your cooperation. I have what I need now."

The man looked up at me with such relief in his one remaining eye, he probably would have clung to my pants like a desperate child if his hands were free.

"Thank you. As I said, I never would have accepted the job if I knew it would affect someone as important as The Wolf. I'll do whatever I can to make up for it."

"Of course you will," I said as I headed for the shack's only door. On my way out, I gave a backhanded order to my security team. "Tie him up and store him in that crate over there. Then, let's go."

As the members of my security immediately followed my orders, I could hear the man struggling behind me.

"Wait. I did as you asked. You can't kill me."

There it was again. People trying to say what I can and can't do.

Stopping on the threshold of the door, I turned back to face him just as my security rustled the man into a metal crate barely big enough to hold him.

I knew all traces of humanity had

vanished from my face. One look at me caused the man to immediately stop fighting and go pale. I'd been told that my "serious face" made me look like a creature from a horror movie that would stalk a person down a dark alley.

"I'm not going to kill you. I'm not sure what will. Maybe the blood loss, or the heat. Maybe you'll just starve to death. But, either way, it won't be my hand that ends you. I can only guarantee my own actions. I can't make promises for the rest of the natural world."

When my people and I finally left the shack, we locked the door behind us. It was an abandoned building in the middle of the desert. No one ever came out here. Based on the state of the place, I had probably been the first person to set foot inside the building in months.

Maybe even years.

Still, for courtesy's sake, it was best to lock the door. We wouldn't want someone to accidentally stumble upon something they shouldn't see, after all.

The afternoon sun beat down upon the earth, baking sand into clay, and I was already on the verge of sweating just from the few minutes I'd spent in the shack.

Thankfully, my driver was competent enough to have the AC in the car already on when I climbed inside.

A brilliant invention, air conditioning. There were people who lived back in the old country who scoffed at others for indulging in such "frivolities", but I would never deny myself the simple luxury of controlled temperature.

There was already enough suffering in the world.

Why endure discomfort when I didn't have to?

"Where to, sir?" the car's driver asked, keeping their words as simple and straightforward as possible so they didn't risk bothering me.

I thought it over for a moment. There was plenty I needed to do and plenty of places I needed to go. I would definitely have to pay Caprice a visit at some point, to let her know her message was received, and it wasn't appreciated.

However, there was only one place I wanted to be right now. Everything else could wait.

"Take me to the *Fantaisiste* office. I need to... inspect the new talent."

CHAPTER NINE

Nathan

The studio was a mess. I'd never actually visited *Fantaisiste's* studio before, but I was certain it hadn't looked like this a few days ago. There were boxes everywhere, to the point it was hard to see the floor. Several mannequins stood off to the side in various stages of assembly, their plastic limbs and heads scattered around like an odd imitation of a murder scene.

Standing at the center of it all was Deacon, surveying everything happening like an Emperor admiring his domain. At his side, in a true reenactment of royalty, Deacon's assistant stood beside him actually controlling everything.

What was her name?

Kiki.

Deacon had insisted that she be hired along with him, and I was now seeing why. He may provide the artistic talent, but she was obviously the one who got things done.

I'd never really had an assistant I could trust like that. There had been times in the past when I had tried, but it never worked out. They all either ended up betraying me, or they couldn't handle living in the shadows, as I preferred. They wanted their position beside someone so powerful to be known, and the lack of recognition led to discontentment and mistakes.

Deacon noticed me after a moment, and even from across the room I could tell there was something off about his reaction to my presence. When I last saw him, we parted on good terms, with an eager anticipation for the future. Now, he almost looked upset, though he tried to hide it.

The hiding was the part that bothered me most. If something had upset him, I wanted to know. Hiding his reaction from me meant that I was likely the cause of his upset.

I couldn't think of anything I'd done that would upset him—at least nothing he would be aware of—and I hated not knowing things. It was like an itch under my skin that couldn't be relieved no matter how hard I scratched.

For a moment, I wondered how to separate Deacon from the chaos surrounding him, but he solved the problem for me. Nodding off to the side in an invitation to follow him, he headed to a door that led to the studio's private office.

As I picked my way between boxes, I heard Kiki delivering orders to the various staff and other designers employed at the studio.

"Careful with that. It's Vicuna. Literally, the rarest fabric in the world. If you damage it, I'll use your skin to replace it."

I couldn't help smiling as I passed. I liked this Kiki woman. If my previous assistants had half her attitude, they might have actually lasted at my side.

I was also glad to see my gift being treated with the care it deserved. That Vicuna fabric had been a present from me to welcome Deacon to his new studio. Not knowing anything about fashion or fabric, I'd simply gone with the rarest, most expensive thing I could find. Thankfully, it seemed to be as impressive as I'd hoped.

Inside the office, there were still a bunch of boxes, but the furniture had been here before Deacon came, and so far, it had remained untouched. Between the desk, the chairs, and the couch, there were plenty of places for Deacon to sit, but he chose to stand in the center of the room with his back to the door. He didn't even turn to face me when I entered the office and closed the door behind me, just remained facing the large window that looked out over the Las Vegas skyline.

"I hope moving to a new studio hasn't been too stressful," I said when it became apparent that Deacon wasn't going to start the conversation.

"No," Deacon said, though his voice was breathy and distracted. "It hasn't been too bad. Honestly, Kiki took care of most of it. I just need to show up and look important."

I approached on light steps. After a lifetime of training, I always moved as if I were stalking an enemy, even when I was trying to be gentle. With Deacon's back to me, and the silence of my footsteps, I felt like a creep intruding where I wasn't wanted.

Deacon was only an arm's length away, close enough for me to touch if I wanted, when he finally spoke up again.

"Someone from Interpol visited me."

He didn't need to say more. I could already guess what had happened.

With a sigh, I took a chance and wrapped my arms around him from behind. "Agent Belden. So, you've met her, too. Charming, isn't she?" Running my lips along the line of his neck, I pressed a quick kiss to his skin." So, what did she accuse me of?"

He flinched within my embrace, but didn't try to pull away, and even tipped his head slightly to the side to give me better access to his neck.

"You already know? Then you realize she's accusing you of killing the model at the show, right?"

I tightened my arm around his waist, pulling him back until our hips pressed together. "Not surprising. Ever since I first met her, she's been determined to lock me up for something. I didn't kill the model, if you were wondering."

Deacon shuddered when I licked the shell of his ear.

"I-I didn't think you did. If there was any evidence proving that you killed her, that Agent would have thrown it in my face when she broke into my studio."

Broke in?

It seemed Agent Belden was determined to sign her own death warrant. Threatening me was one thing. Threatening someone harmless like Deacon was an entirely different matter. Until now, I'd considered her a nuisance at worst. Something I could easily ignore. However, it seemed I was going to need to take care of her in a more permanent way. Especially, since she had no interest in doing her real job. Considering how easy it had been to locate the actual killer, Agent Belden wasn't interested in solving a murder. She just wanted an excuse to get to me.

Deacon's hand tangled in my hair and pressed my face deeper against his neck. I could practically taste the beat of his pulse.

"It wasn't the murder accusation that bothered me. Although, I didn't like being called an accessory to murder. No, what really bothered me was how casual the accusation was. Like killing people is a common occurrence for you."

This was a dangerous topic of conversation that hit too close to the truth. I needed to distract Deacon, but if I changed the topic too quickly or denied the accusation too vehemently, it would seem suspicious.

Instead, I leaned into the topic, over-exaggerating to make the very idea seem ridiculous.

Letting my hand slowly creep downward, I whispered directly into his ear. "What if it was? What if I was a killer with a body count in the hundreds? What would you do then? Would you run away?"

When he didn't stop me, I dipped the tips of my fingers inside the waistband of his pants.

"Or, would the thrill of sleeping with a killer excite you?" I slid my hand all the way inside his pants. "Based on how hard you are now, I think I know what the answer would be."

"Fuuuuck," Deacon groaned as I started stroking his cock over his underwear. "You're such a... tease."

I abruptly stopped the movement of my hand. "Tease? Hardly. A tease makes promises without delivering on them."

Pulling my hand out of his pants, I wrapped both arms around him and picked him up just enough to drag him over to the couch. He ended up sitting in my lap with his back pressed against my chest.

"I can't be a tease, because I fully intend to fulfill my promises."

All thoughts of murder investigations and Interpol were forgotten as I freed him from his pants and shirt. Conscious of his anxiety around sex, I left his underwear in place. The barrier between full skin contact seemed to help relieve his worries, for although he was obviously nervous, he didn't try to stop me.

In fact, he only made one demand as he sat nearly naked in my lap.

"Call me Deke. My full name has always sounded weird. There are too many religious connections to that word."

Considering all the trust he was placing in my hands, using his preferred nickname could hardly even be considered a favor. It was just general respect. I understood the importance of a name, considering the fact that I'd changed mine as well.

With one hand, I tipped his chin back and to the side, so he was in a better position to be kissed. Sitting on my lap like this, if he were any taller it wouldn't have worked, but our respective sizes fit perfectly.

Meanwhile, I stroked my other hand up the inside of his thigh, brushing against the arousal trapped within his underwear. He was so hard that the thin cloth couldn't fully contain him, and the flash of intimate skin was almost more tantalizing than if he'd been fully naked.

As I tugged at the band of his underwear, Deke suddenly grabbed my hand and pulled his mouth free from my kiss.

"How..." He was still panting, struggling to regain his breath after I practically sucked it out of him. "How far are you going?"

"Don't worry," I reassured him as I nipped the skin behind his ear. "We'll only do what you're comfortable with. For now, we're definitely not going all the way. We're just trying out something new."

Deke let go of my hand, but he was still looking down at his mostly naked state and my hands on his body with a concerned expression. "But, what about you?"

"What do you mean?"

I cupped the heated flesh between his legs, and he squirmed on my lap, unintentionally grinding his ass back against my own throbbing arousal. If I didn't know better, I'd think he was purposely taunting me with what I couldn't have.

"This seems unfair," he finally explained when he stopped squirming enough to speak. "I'm getting all the attention. How is this any fun for you?"

My grip on him instinctively tightened, and I was on the verge of leaving bruises on his skin. "Are you worried about my pleasure?"

"Yeah." His voice was even more breathless than before. Being held tighter seemed to excite him. "I'm used to... giving more than receiving, you know?"

I didn't even have to read between the lines to know what he was saying. His previous lovers had focused only on their own pleasure, and since Deke couldn't give them what they wanted, he had to do extra work to compensate.

That changed today.

"Watching you lost in pleasure is its own kind of enjoyment. But if you want us to both participate... then I have another idea."

Keeping an arm around him, I used one hand to open my own pants just enough to expose my cock to open air. Deke was facing away from me, so he couldn't see exactly what I was doing, but he could obviously tell from my movements, because he started squirming with nerves rather than pleasure.

"What... um, what are you doing?"

"Don't worry." I pressed several kisses against his throat. "We aren't going to do anything you aren't ready for. Just follow my lead."

Coaxing him with gentle hands and even gentler words, I guided him to press his thighs tightly together, then slid my cock between them. It wasn't as good as actually being inside him, but the squeeze of warm, soft flesh around my already sensitive shaft still brought a thrill of pleasure running though my veins.

With small jerks of his hips, almost as

if I were fucking him, I slid my cock in and out between his thighs.

"Oh, this." He sighed, sounding disappointed. "I've done this before."

That wasn't the reaction I wanted. Without stopping the thrust of my hips, I also wrapped a hand around his cock and started stroking him with synchronized movements.

He shrieked, obviously not expecting the sudden rush of pleasure. "Ah, this is—" His voice cut off as I rubbed my thumb over the head of his cock, causing his back to arch. "It's... actually good."

"Don't be so surprised." When he arched, he also squeezed his legs tighter together, making me gasp as well. "Your previous partners were too simple-minded. They had no idea what they were doing."

He was the perfect combination of hard and soft. His skin was supple and pliant, but he was also tanned and toned from plenty of outdoor activity. He yielded just the perfect amount to my touch.

As we both neared our completion, I used my free hand to tip his head back into another kiss. I pushed my tongue into his mouth, sealing my lips over his and swallowing every desperate sound he made as his whole body trembled.

We came at nearly the same time, clinging desperately together. His nails dug into my forearms, the only part of me he could easily reach, and would have drawn blood if I wasn't clothed.

My own hips jerked against him, trying to drive my cock deeper into the cradle of his thighs as the pleasure of climax exploded along my nerves.

We were breathing too hard to maintain the kiss, but we didn't separate, just simply breathed against each other's mouths as we rode through the final waves of orgasm. It took a few minutes to calm down, but even then we stayed tightly embraced.

Deacon's voice ghosted over my skin, more air than actual sound. "I've never actually enjoyed that before."

His hair was slightly damp with sweat when I nuzzled against his temple. "Like I said, your previous partners were too simpleminded. No imagination."

"I feel like I've been cheated. Although..." He looked down at himself. The results of both his own pleasure and mine splattered over his stomach and thighs. "It's still just as much of a mess as always."

Pressing one last kiss to his temple, I urged him off the couch. "Luckily, this office has its own bathroom. Let me help you get cleaned up."

The bathroom fortunately had a shower, but there was only enough space for one at a time. However, my disappointment of not being able to share the shower was tempered by the enjoyment of watching Deacon through the rising steam. The sight of hot water running over his every muscle and curve was enough to get me excited again, and I was already planning what to do with him next.

Not right now. There was only so much we could do in an office with an entire staff of people just on the other side of the door. My plans would have to wait until later, when I coaxed him into the privacy of my bedroom.

My resolve to wait was tested as I showered as well. Deacon didn't even try to hide how closely he watched me. He even insisted on helping me dry off, taking much more time than necessary to run the towel over every inch of my body.

His attention was sparked by my tattoos, though he didn't ask about them. They ran from my neck all the way to my wrists, covering most of my torso. Each one had a specific meaning.

Maybe someday, I'd be able to tell him about them.

By the time I was dressed again, I was nearly convinced to throw caution out the window and claim him on the office floor.

However, just as I reached for him again, we were interrupted by the sound of sudden high-pitched screaming that rang out from the main studio area.

CHAPTER TEN

Deacon

The screaming cut off abruptly, but the sudden silence was even more terrifying. My heart pounded in my ears. Nathan and I charged through the office door into the workshop.

So much chaos greeted us, it was impossible to tell what had happened. The studio staff and other designers, who I'd only just met, were running around in confusion like a swarm of bees whose hive had been kicked. Even their babbling sounded like the unintelligible buzz of insects.

I considered grabbing the nearest

person and demanding to know what had happened, but Nathan shouldered past everyone into the center of the room. Two people lay on the floor. A designer I had met but couldn't remember her name, and...

"Kiki!"

I rushed to my fallen friend, but Nathan held me back.

"Nathan? What the fuck? Let me go."

"Wait." His voice was too calm for the situation, almost intimate as he spoke directly into my ear. I was on the verge of shouting at him, when he picked up a nearby clothing hook and used it to prod a roll of fabric lying between the two women.

"Do you smell that?"

Startled by the unexpected question, I automatically took a deep breath through my nose.

"I don't smell anything."

"Pyrenic. It's like arsenic, but... more."

"What does that mean?" I asked as I watched him use the clothing hook to move the fabric to an isolated spot on the floor.

"That fabric is poisoned."

"What? But— That's not..." I sputtered,

not sure what I was even trying to say.

While I was still trying to get my brain working, Nathan had already taken charge. He ordered someone to call for an ambulance while also making sure no one touched the fabric or the women. He then immediately started questioning everyone about what happened, quickly getting a summary of events.

Kiki and the other designer had been taking stock of our supplies. The other designer had taken the fabric out of its box, and Kiki had come over to chastise her since it was a particularly expensive material. After a few moments, the other designer collapsed. Panic set in and people started screaming. Kiki had tried to calm things down, but before anyone could figure out what happened, she collapsed as well.

The shock of seeing a second person suddenly go limp had shocked people into silence, which was when Nathan and I entered.

I listened to this explanation with a blank expression. Everything felt fuzzy, like I was merely watching a scene in a movie rather than walking through real life.

Meanwhile, Nathan handled everything with efficiency, and kept people from panicking again as we waited for the ambulance to arrive.

He was too calm. Surely, in this situation, even someone as confident as him should be panicking a little bit.

My mind turned over and over, like a hamster running frantically on a wheel but not getting anywhere. Before I could successfully collect my thoughts and get them moving forward again, paramedics arrived along with the police.

Nathan explained the situation to the paramedics, who whisked Kiki and the other designer away. The police, however, hung around to question people and get an account of the incident.

That was when things started to get weird.

The police were conducting interrogations, as they should, yet they barely spoke to the people who had actually been present. Instead, they focused almost entirely on Nathan.

The man had three police officers standing around him, bombarding him with questions from all sides. He could barely get out a few words to answer one question before he was interrupted by another.

It looked like a group of cats batting a mouse back and forth, except this mouse refused to budge. No matter how insistent or annoying the police officers were, Nathan maintained his usual composure.

Curious, and a little suspicious, I crept closer to eavesdrop on the uneven conversation.

"You bought that cloth, didn't you, Mister Sterling?" one of the police officers asked.

With a slight nod of his head that still kept his eyeline above the officer's, Nathan agreed. "I did. I own the company. You'll find that I funded most of the supplies here."

The officers weren't dissuaded, and immediately jumped in with another question. "Yes, but you specifically sought this fabric out personally. Why?"

Since all three officers were asking him questions at the same time, Nathan didn't bother trying to look at them individually. He only addressed the officer standing in front of him, as if they were having a private conversation.

"Vicuna fabric is rare and hard to find.

It was meant as a gift, so it had to be perfect."

Right. The Vicuna fabric. I'd forgotten about that. It had been a gift from Nathan to celebrate moving into the new studio. Kiki had been gushing about it just that morning.

The officers couldn't seriously be suggesting that Nathan had gifted the fabric specifically to poison it.

Could they?

That didn't even make sense. If he wanted to poison anyone here, he had plenty of opportunities. He wouldn't need to use such a dramatic method.

That was when the reality of the situation finally hit me. This hadn't been an accident. Fabric didn't accidentally end up laced with poison.

Someone had harmed Kiki intentionally. Even if she wasn't their target, she had been harmed because someone chose to do so.

The fuzzy unreality in my head was clearing up, but it was replaced with too sharp clarity. My vision tunneled, and I could practically count every speck of dust floating through a nearby ray of sunlight streaming through the window. I could hear every nervous shuffle of the officers' feet as they continued their interrogation, and the lack of any fidgeting or nervous gestures coming from Nathan.

A phone rang, shrill and sharp, and the sound bounced painfully off my eardrums. I flinched, but I still heard every word one of the officers said as they answered the phone.

"Hello. Yes. Really? I see. I'm sorry to hear that. Yes, we'll be in to see the body soon."

With a beep, the call disconnected. The officer turned back to Nathan with a smirk on their face that they were trying to hide.

"That was the hospital. One of the women died in the ambulance on the way there. This is it, Sterling. You're looking at a murder charge."

Nathan didn't even flinch. He simply reminded them that whoever had poisoned the fabric was guilty of murder, but since he hadn't been the one to poison it, he wouldn't be the one arrested.

I barely heard a word he said. The officer's previous statement rang in my head.

One of the women died.

My legs went numb, and I collapsed to the floor, knocking over a half-assembled mannequin and creating a cacophony of noise.

"Deke." Nathan shoved past the officers to kneel beside me, finally looking upset for the first time. "Are you okay?"

"Kiki…"

I couldn't say more than that. Even her name barely left my lips. Yet, Nathan luckily understood what I meant.

"I'm sure Kiki isn't dead." Wrapping an arm around my shoulder, he pulled me closer. "I heard the paramedics say that she didn't get as big a dose of the poison. I'm sure she'll be fine."

A surge of frantic energy burned through my veins, my hands moving seemingly without the input of my brain, and I latched onto Nathan's lapel.

"I need to go to the hospital. I need to see her."

Nathan carefully grabbed my hands and removed them from the fabric but didn't push me away. "Okay. We'll go." Helping me stand, he looked over at the officers with a stern expression. "I assume we're done here."

One of the officers stepped forward, closely flanked by the other two. "We still have more questions. For you, and..." The officer trailed off, and whispered to one of the others, who answered in an equally hushed tone. "For you, and Mister Millar as well. You'll both need to come down to the station."

I opened my mouth to argue, the words halfway off my tongue, when Nathan squeezed my shoulder to silence me.

"Are you arresting us?" he asked.

None of the officers said anything, but the looks on their faces were answer enough.

Sighing, Nathan led me toward the door. "If you aren't arresting us, then we don't have to come with you. I've already answered your questions. If there's anything else you need to know, we can come down to the station later. For now, we're needed elsewhere."

If the officers tried to stop us, I never knew. Nathan practically marched me out of the studio and slammed the door behind us before I heard another word from the officers. Keeping an arm around my shoulder, he brought me to a car in the parking lot that had a driver waiting next to it.

At first, I thought he'd called an Uber when I wasn't looking, but once we were inside the car and Nathan addressed the driver personally, I realized this wasn't hired transportation. This was Nathan's personal car and personal driver.

Is this what it was like being rich?

Paying someone to specifically wait around and be ready to take you anywhere you needed to go at the drop of a hat?

It seemed a little weird, but it was also very convenient. We were able to get to the hospital with minimal hassle.

My feet carried me through the building's sterile hallways like I was gliding rather than walking. I didn't remember taking a single step. I didn't even remember asking the nurse at the front desk for Kiki's room, but soon enough, I found myself standing at the foot of her hospital bed.

There were a bunch of wires and tubes hooked up to her, and her face looked much more pale and gaunt than it had that morning. Only a few hours had made such a difference to her appearance. Even her blonde curls seemed to hang limp on her head.

Her makeup was also horribly smudged. Mascara streaked from the corner of her eyes, creating artificial crow's feet, and her lipstick was so mucky her mouth looked like it was about to fall off her face.

She would hate being seen this way.

After my very first job working with models, I'd started keeping makeup wipes in my pocket at all times. It came in handy now as I sat beside her bed and started cleaning up her face. I wished I had new makeup to apply, so she could look as perfect as usual when she woke up, but at this point a bare face would still be better than the mess she currently wore.

Nathan didn't immediately follow me into the room, and instead, stayed out in the hall talking to a doctor. I'd cleaned off most of Kiki's makeup by the time he stepped inside, though he stayed near the wall to give us space.

"The doctor said that she must not have handled the fabric very much, because the dose of poison she received wasn't very high. The poison was extremely concentrated, so it still affected her, but they expect she should recover just fine in a few days."

I nodded, relieved, but I still couldn't bear to look away from her.

"We met in high school." I laughed, only to find tears filling my eyes and a lump clogging my throat. "The only two gay kids in a very conservative school. We were each other's beards for years."

Heavy silence emanated from Nathan's corner of the room.

"Beard?"

He said the word like he was turning over each letter, looking for a hidden message. It made his accent, usually so faint it was barely noticeable, stand out much more prominently.

"I know the word but... I'm afraid I don't know this term."

I laughed again, and wiped my cheeks clear of tears that hadn't fallen in the first place. "I mean, that we pretended to date each other in order to pose as a straight couple and hide the fact that we were gay. We fake-dated all through high school. Even when I got a boyfriend, she covered for me. Then, when we graduated, we left it all behind and moved to Las Vegas.

Religious families. College funds. Easy lives where everything was already decided. We gave it all up to live freely in the city of sin."

The first tear finally fell. Once the dam broke, I expected more to come, but they didn't. That single tear carved a lonely path down my cheek as I finally looked away from Kiki to stare up at Nathan.

"I don't have anyone else. She's all I've got, and someone tried to kill her."

The tears that hadn't fallen still sat behind my eyes, boiling hot as they slowly changed from sadness to rage.

Stepping out of his corner, Nathan placed a hand on my shoulder. "I doubt she was the target. Whoever poisoned the fabric was likely just trying to hurt as many people as possible in order to sabotage the company."

Acid burned the back of my throat and my teeth ached with excess emotion as I slapped his hand away.

"I don't care if she wasn't the target. She's the one who was hurt. If she'd picked up that fabric first, instead of that other designer, she'd be... she'd be..."

I couldn't say it, but that didn't stop the image from flashing behind my eyes anyway.

Kiki lying on a morgue table instead of a hospital bed, her face gray and lifeless.

It was only a stroke of luck that I was listening to a beeping heart monitor right now, instead of a flatline.

As if triggered by my thoughts, Kiki's heart monitor started wailing an alarm. I jumped in panic, afraid that my imagination had been brought to life and she was dying right in front of my eyes.

Only seconds after the heart monitor started wailing, a nurse bustled into the room.

"What's the... Oh. I see."

All the worry slid off her face, and she calmly walked over to the side of the bed and started messing with the various tubes and wires.

"Sir. You're going to need to let go. You've pulled the heart monitor off."

Looking down at my hands, I realized it was true. I'd been subconsciously holding onto Kiki's hand. When I got upset, I'd held tighter, accidentally dislodging the heart monitor that had been clipped to her finger.

I jumped off the bed and nearly crashed into the nurse in the process.

"Sorry. I didn't mean... Fuck. I'm sorry."

Kiki had almost died, and here I was only hurting her more. Logically, in the back of my mind, I knew that removing the heart monitor hadn't actually done any harm. The nurse clipped it back on, and the wailing monitor fell silent. Yet, I couldn't silence the whisper in my brain that blamed me for her condition. For that moment, when the heart monitor stopped, it felt like her heart had stopped as well, and I'd been the one to stop it.

My feet pounded against the linoleum floor as I ran from the room. Nathan called my name, but I didn't even slow down. I ran until I reached the end of the hallway. My momentum sent me bouncing off the wall. I stumbled but remained upright and kept running in a different direction.

There was no telling how long or far I ran. Every hospital I'd ever seen was a twisted labyrinth of white walls and misleading signs. This one was no different. I could have been on the other side of the compound, or I could have been only a few rooms down from where I started. There was no way to know.

I passed an open door to an empty

room, and making a quick decision, I slipped inside and slammed the door behind me.

It was dark, and after the bright lights of the hospital hallway, my eyes needed a moment to adjust. Once I was able to see, I found myself in what appeared to be a break room. It was empty at the moment, but there was an old moth-eaten couch on one side, and a table with a few chairs on the other. A refrigerator hummed away in one corner, while a sink holding a stack of drying coffee mugs on its adjoining small counter sat on the opposite wall.

I stood, unmoving in the dim atmosphere, my breath coming in short little pants. Even after my heart rate calmed down after my sudden sprint, I couldn't seem to get my breathing under control.

The door behind me opened. I hadn't known Nathan for that long, but his footsteps were easily recognizable from the way he made almost no sound when he moved.

"Deke. Are you all right?"

I didn't answer. My breathing came even more erratically, and something bitter settled like a ball in my stomach, pushing up on my breastbone until it felt like my heart would be smashed against my ribs.

"Fuck!"

I grabbed one of the chairs from the table and threw it against the wall. With a resounding crash, one of the legs broke off and it left a deep hole in the drywall.

Picking up the now three-legged chair, I smashed it several more times against the floor. "Fuck. Fuck. Fuck."

Someone came into the room, demanding to know what was going on, but Nathan quickly intercepted them. I never heard what he said, but a moment later, he convinced them to leave, then he closed and locked the door so we were alone.

"Deke," he started to say, but I cut him off.

Grabbing his lapel, I pulled him forward, so our faces were only inches apart.

"Who are you?"

Nathan held both hands out to his side, almost like he was surrendering. "I'm not sure what you mean."

Gritting my teeth, I tried to shake him

by my grip on his jacket, but the man was infuriatingly solid and didn't budge.

"I'm not an idiot, Nathan. I see the signs. When Agent Belden showed up at my old studio to question me about that model who was killed, she made a lot of insinuations about you."

"I told you," Nathan said as he placed a gentle yet firm hand on my wrists. "Agent Belden has a vendetta against me. She'll accuse me of anything she can think of."

I held firm to his jacket, though I stopped trying to shake him. It wasn't accomplishing anything.

"That's actually even more suspicious. Most people don't have regular interactions with Interpol. And today, those officers were only interested in questioning you. Why? You weren't even in the room when the poisoning happened."

"I did buy the fabric," Nathan tried to reason.

"That's not enough. Those officers had already decided it was you from the moment they showed up. Was that due to Agent Belden's vendetta as well?"

He barely reacted as I practically

shouted at him, and was far too calm when he replied. "Probably. You're right that they were ready to arrest me. I suspect Agent Belden probably put them up to it. Or maybe even blatantly lied to them. It wouldn't be the first time."

He wasn't listening to me. His hazel eyes had hardened into a steel wall, completely shutting me out. I realized that he wasn't going to tell me anything. He was barely even listening to me. We could talk all day, and he would keep spinning the conversation in unhelpful circles.

"You're too calm. This whole time, you've been too calm. You weren't even surprised by the sight of someone dying right in front of you. Normal people are upset by things like that, but it was just an ordinary thing to you."

"Are you... blaming me for keeping my composure?"

Letting go of his jacket, I shoved as hard as I could against his chest. A small flame of pride lit within my heart when I managed to knock him off balance and he had to take a step back.

"No. I'm saying that all these things together are too suspicious. I'm no genius, but I'm also not stupid. There's something going on, and you're at the center of it. So, tell me who you are and what's actually happening here."

Still keeping a straight face, Nathan fixed the rumpled lapel of his jacket. "You don't need to worry about anything. It'll be handled, and I promise that you and your friend will be safe."

He turned to leave, and that hard bitter thing in my stomach erupted. Fury bubbled up within me and erupted like a volcano, driving my hands and voice to act on their own.

"Listen to me, damn it." I was shouting now, but it had no more effect on Nathan than if I'd whispered.

Trembling so badly that my teeth chattered, I shoved his shoulder. Then, when he finally turned back to look at me, I slapped him across the face hard enough for his head to snap to the side.

"Don't dismiss me like I'm a child."

He stood there with his head turned to the side for longer than necessary. His hands clenched into fists at his sides, but for several moments he didn't move.

I probably should have left, or at least apologized, but I did neither. Instead, I waited in silence for his reaction, equal parts smug and angry.

When he finally did look at me, his expression was slightly surprised, like he couldn't believe what had just happened. However, that surprise was quickly replaced with a dark predatory look, the likes of which I'd never seen before.

He stalked toward me, and I stumbled backward. My feet hit the edge of the couch and I fell, landing sprawled over the cushions.

Nathan didn't give me a chance to find my feet again. He knelt over me, literally straddling my lap, and gripped the back of the couch so his larger body completely caged me in. With one hand, he gripped under my chin, fingers digging into each of my cheeks as he forced me to look up at him.

"For someone who claims he isn't stupid, that was a very stupid thing to do."

I really needed to learn how to censor myself, but without Kiki to act as my filter, I completely lacked impulse control.

"Is that a threat?" With him holding my face in such a tight grip, my cheeks were pushed forward like I was pouting, and my words were slurred. It wasn't a very intimidating expression, but I scowled up at him anyway.

He was breathing heavily through his nose, and I noticed tremors in his hand as he struggled to maintain his usual composure.

"I'm not threatening you." He leaned a little closer, so our foreheads almost touched, but it didn't feel like an intimate gesture. "Now, listen to me. I did not kill that model at your show. I did not kill that designer today, and I did not hurt your friend."

Even I was surprised by the smile that twisted my lips.

"You know, most people, when proclaiming their innocence, would just say that they haven't killed anyone. But... that would be a lie, wouldn't it. You have. Just not in these specific instances."

He let go of my face but didn't let me off the couch.

I leaned forward so our foreheads did touch. "So, are you going to tell me what's going on now, or do I have to keep guessing?"

Nathan's hand hovered in the minimal air between us, hesitating like he wasn't sure what to do with it. For a moment, it seemed like he might grab me by the throat, but instead, all he did was lay his palm over my heart.

"You're lucky I like you. Anyone else who tried to threaten me like this wouldn't get a second chance. But I'm warning you. Stop."

The moth-eaten couch didn't have much padding left. When I threw my head back and laughed, I knocked my skull against the hard wooden frame.

"Now who's the one being stupid?"

For the first time, Nathan looked truly shocked. Not mildly surprised or confused as I'd seen before, but genuinely shocked.

Seeing such an unusual expression on his face made me grin with a sense of accomplishment. "I'm not trying to threaten you. I don't care what you've done. I don't care if you actually have killed people. I just want to know what's going on and who hurt Kiki."

I watched Nathan take a deep breath, obviously struggling for the composure that usually came so easily to him.

"I... may know who is behind this. And I assure you, it'll be taken care of. You don't need to worry. Now, its best if you leave it alone and stop asking questions you don't want the answers to."

Hitting Nathan again would be pointless, and in this position, nearly impossible, but that didn't stop the urge. I balled my hands into fists and they itched with the desire to lash out, but instead I only glared up at him.

"Don't tell me what I do and don't want. Don't make those decisions for me like I'm not capable of deciding for myself. If you have any respect for me, you'll tell me what I want to know."

"And then what?" Nathan snapped. His hand balled into a fist against my shirt, crinkling the fabric between his fingers. "Even if I do tell you, what good will it do?"

I laughed. It probably sounded manic, but I didn't care.

"Good? Probably not any good. I don't think you're a good man. That's fine. I don't need a good man right now. I need an efficient one." When I grinned at him, my expression showed too many teeth. It wasn't a happy expression, which made sense. I wasn't feeling particularly happy at the moment.

Truthfully, I wasn't sure what I was feeling.

Anger?

Yes. But there was also a whole host of other things swirling around in my chest that I couldn't pick apart.

All I knew was that I needed to move. Needed to act. I wouldn't be satisfied with just sitting back and letting other people handle things for me.

"You're going to take down the person who hurt Kiki," I said with complete certainty. "And when you do, I'm going to be there with you."

CHAPTER ELEVEN

Nathan

Not once, in my forty-six years of life, had I ever divulged a secret I didn't mean to tell. When my parents questioned me about my grandmother's broken vase, I said nothing. Hours of police interrogation had never gotten a single bit of incriminating evidence out of me. Even torture, which I had experienced only once during my earlier days as a Mafia boss, failed to have any effect.

So, it was a complete surprise when, upon saying that he wanted to personally make the people who hurt his friend pay, I ended up telling Deacon the truth about myself.

Not the entire truth. I still kept some secrets to myself. He didn't know that I was the actual leader of the Chechen Mafia, but he now knew that I was an important member of it.

He also didn't care. Or at least, he pretended that he didn't care. I wasn't sure if his nonchalant acceptance was real, or if it was just a symptom of his friend's near-death experience. I still suspected that, once Kiki was well and her poisoner dealt with, the reality of the situation might finally catch up with Deacon and he would realize what he'd gotten himself into. However, for now, he sat beside me in a first-class airplane seat, watching the clouds out the window like he was just enjoying an average trip.

"Why don't you have a private jet?" he asked suddenly.

The stewardess had already come around to serve drinks, and I held a glass of whiskey that was more ice-melt than alcohol. I'd hoped it would help settle me, but it didn't. For the first time in as long as I could remember, I felt wrong-footed, and I couldn't figure out how to find my balance again. The longer Deacon continued to act as though everything were normal, the more unsettled I felt.

"A private jet? No, I don't have one. Why do you ask?"

With a shrug, Deacon closed the window shutter to block out the sunlight that reflected off the top of the clouds. "In movies and stuff, people..." His eyes darted around as he glanced briefly at the other passengers of the plane. In first class there was more space between the seats, but we still had no privacy. "People... in your position, always have their own private jets."

"People in my position?"

It felt strange to make jokes about something I usually worked so hard to keep secret. My tongue tripped over my words, and I sarcastically turned his own phrase back on him just to hide the fact that I didn't know what to say.

"Yeah. You know." Deacon smirked and looked up at me through his lashes. "Big boss man."

He started laughing, and I couldn't help chuckling a little as well, though in the back of my mind, I worried. I hadn't told him that I was the leader of my family, so his use of the word "boss" was likely just meant as a joke, but I still wondered if he'd somehow figured out more than I meant to tell him. He'd already convinced me to reveal my secrets to him. At this point, it wouldn't surprise me to learn that he'd uncovered even more than I meant for him to know.

Pushing away the worry, I leaned back in my chair and forced myself to act casual.

"Owning a private jet really isn't worth the effort. The plane doesn't go any faster, and it's a waste to burn so much fuel just to transport me. Usually, first class is good enough, though on the rare occasion when a public plane isn't good enough, I can always rent a private jet, if needed."

Deacon's gaze flickered up and down my figure. "Hmmm. An environmentally responsible criminal mastermind, I see."

Ever since learning the truth about who I am, he'd been in a strange mood. He was fidgety, like he had too much energy running through his veins. The unusual attitude contributed to my worry. I could tell there was a thought in his head that he hadn't come to terms with, and feared what would happen when he finally did. However, until I could determine where we actually stood with each other, I would have to continue moving forward with my plans.

The world didn't stop turning just because I was having an off day, and my enemies certainly wouldn't give me a break to deal with personal issues.

Deacon's face suddenly appeared right in front of me. I'd been so wrapped up in my thoughts, I hadn't noticed him leaning over from his seat to stare at me.

His finger rubbed at the crease between my brows. "You seem worried. What's wrong?"

I couldn't admit that he was the thing worrying me.

What would I even say?

Stop acting so normal. Now that you know who I am, you're supposed to be scared and disgusted with me.

I didn't want such a thing to be true, and I didn't want to accidentally wish it into existence by saying it out loud.

Instead, I gave him a different explanation. While not accurate, it was still true.

"I'm wondering how the fabric was poisoned in the first place. That kind of Vicuna fabric was hard to find. I had to call in a favor with some personal contacts to get my hands on it so quickly. It was in either my possession, or the possession of someone I trust, almost the entire time. So how could the poisoner have gotten access to it?"

Deacon finally looked worried as he considered what I'd said, but after only a moment, he returned to lounging in his own seat.

"I don't really know how any of this works, but it seems to me that we'll just have to ask the guy once we find him."

He suddenly sat up from his relaxed pose and pinned me with a stern eye. "You are going to let me be there when you confront him, right?"

Deacon claimed that he wanted to personally take revenge for his friend, but did he really understand what that meant?

When we found the poisoner, the guy wasn't going to tell us what we wanted to know. I would likely have to extract the information I wanted by force.

How would Deacon react once he saw the blood on my hands with his own eyes?

The flight from Las Vegas to New York

was less than five hours, so before we knew it, we were climbing into a car waiting for us in front of the JFK airport.

"So, where are we going?" Deacon asked as he watched the tall buildings passing by the window.

Las Vegas was hardly a small city, but it was more of a sprawling structure of glitter and neon. New York was just as impressive in its own, different way. In the heart of the city, the buildings stood so tall the sky seemed like a forgotten memory, and the only way to see the expanse of blue was to crane your neck and stare straight up.

A police car drove past, going in the opposite direction to us. The inside of our car turned red and blue for a moment, then the siren faded into the distance. I waited for it to pass and for silence to fall again—or at least as silent as a major city ever got—and gave Deacon a basic explanation of what to expect.

During the five-hour flight, my contact in New York City had been busy. As soon as I agreed to take care of Caprice Vidales for D'Angelo, my first step had been to place a spy within the Vidales organization. I'd only wanted someone to keep an eye on things, but this spy had gone above and beyond, and managed to earn a place as Caprice Vidales's secretary.

I'd have to give my spy a raise, because thanks to her efforts, I knew exactly where Caprice was at all times and exactly what the woman was doing. This is why I not only knew she was in New York, but exactly in which office building I could find her.

I also knew she was scheduled to meet with a member of her family who was well known among criminal circles as a hitman.

Poisoning the fabric at the studio had been a sophisticated tactic. Definitely the work of a professional. Their method should have worked. None one employed at the studio would have recognized the poisoned fabric for what it was, and it could have killed a lot of people before they realized what happened. Even the paramedics may not have realized the cause, and could have been poisoned as well.

Unfortunately for Caprice's sabotage plans, I'd decided to make an impromptu visit to the studio in order to see Deacon, and I ended up putting a stop to their plan before it could do too much harm.

Caprice had to be seething right now, to learn that all her efforts had only resulted in the death of a single assistant designer whose absence wouldn't affect *Fantaisiste* in any way.

Our car pulled to a stop in an alley behind the building.

"You're going in alone?" Deacon asked as I held the door open for him.

"Of course not," I said with a smile. "You're here."

I could see the concern on his face, and wondered if this was the moment he would realize what he was about to walk into, but a moment later, he steeled his resolve and stepped out of the car.

"Don't worry," I assured him as I closed the car door. "I've brought my own security. They're already in place and just waiting for me."

The door into the building had no visible security. There was a camera over the doorframe, but I had faith that my own people had already taken care of it. They wouldn't be my people if they weren't competent enough to take care of something so simple.

So, I strolled through the back door with ease and stepped into the reception area from the rear. The security stationed there was obviously surprised by my sudden appearance, but like true professionals, they didn't bother to even question me before pointing their weapons in my direction.

Deacon grabbed by arm, understandably scared to be staring down the barrels of multiple guns. No matter how gung-ho he seemed about the situation, nothing could prepare someone for the first time they faced a weapon that could kill them with less effort than it took to sneeze.

Just as I'd promised, my security was already in position. Appearing out of seemingly nowhere, they took down the armed guards like silent shadows. Not a single bullet was fired, and no one was killed yet. The guards were simply restrained for now. My people knew better than to start killing until I'd given permission for lethal force. My main goal was always to keep a low profile, and that meant not leaving a string of bodies everywhere I went and resorting to deadly measures only when necessary.

I had no qualms against killing, but I always made it count when I did.

The guards in the front lobby weren't the building's only security. We ran into nearly a dozen guards on our way to the top floor.

By the elevator.

In the elevator.

Guarding the stairs.

Standing sentry on the top floor.

They were everywhere. Caprice was not taking any chances.

My people took care of every guard we came across with the same efficiency as the first ones, and my path to Caprice's office was left unhindered.

"You've gotten paranoid in your old age, Caprice," I said as I entered the office. "Not losing your touch, are you?"

The woman sitting behind the desk wasn't even that old. Late thirties, at most. As someone well into their forties, I had no room to talk, but I knew the comment would piss her off.

She sneered at me, tapping her sharp red nails against the top of her desk. "What is this? The Wolf has his own pet now? Are you taking it for a walk?"

Some people, like D'Angelo, knew my

name. I suspected that man might even know my real name. Caprice knew the name Nathan Sterling, but she didn't know my original name, and I could tell it bothered her. The way she insisted on using my moniker, her lip twisting in displeasure over the word, made it obvious how much she hated being out of the loop.

The fact that D'Angelo and Caprice were both leaders within the Italian Mafia, yet there was such a difference in their information, was telling. Caprice was the head of the Vidales family, but she didn't control the entire Italian Mafia. She was a lord who imagined herself as a king, and it gave her too much confidence.

A pair of women stood behind Caprice, armed to the teeth, and ready to spring into action at a moment's notice. Her personal bodyguards were specially picked, and very lethal.

Unfortunately for them, so was I.

A man sat on the other side of the desk, unremarkable except for the twisted scar just above his left eye. According to my spy's information, this was the hitman who had poisoned my employees.

I nodded toward him. "Your man here

missed. I'm not dead. Neither is my company. I'm surprised you thought that would work."

Caprice scoffed. "I'm not foolish enough to think such a simple thing could kill you. That was merely to send a message."

I felt Deacon grow tense at my side as he realized the man sitting just a few feet away was the one who had killed one of the other designers and hurt Kiki.

To distract everyone else in the room from Deacon, I took another step forward, so he was partially behind me.

"And what message is that?"

"That I know what you're up to. You never had any interest in my business before. You're only trying to compete with me because that spoiled brat asked you to get me off his back so he can deal with his little Russian friends."

She really was bold if she considered the Russians to be 'little'. Even I would hesitate before getting involved with them. Her arrogance was starting to get on my nerves.

Her bodyguards seemed to sense my shift in mood, for their hands drifted toward their nearest weapons. "D'Angelo is the same age as you. Hardly a brat."

"Well, he acts like one." She still hadn't risen from the desk, and her unconcerned attitude was starting to make the other people in the room twitchy. Tension was growing with every word we exchanged, and something was going to snap soon.

I shifted so Deacon was positioned a little more behind me.

Caprice's gaze zeroed in on the gesture.

"You know. I'm surprised you came in person. All I did was kill a civilian who happened to be employed by your new company. That shouldn't be worth your personal time." She nodded toward Deacon. "Are you showing off for your new pet or is there another reason you brought him along?"

She was right. Such a minor infraction against me usually wouldn't be worth my time. The only reason it mattered so much to me was because it mattered so much to Deacon. I was giving too much information about our relationship away simply by being here.

Why had I brought Deacon with me?

Confronting Caprice on my own was already unnecessary. Bringing Deacon along just because he demanded it was borderline insanity.

The only reason I could come up with is that I was curious. He wanted to get revenge for his friend with his own hands, and claimed he was fine with my real identity. I wasn't used to people not being afraid of me. Even Caprice's attitude at that very moment was more show than truth. She was putting on a brave face, but Deacon didn't need to be brave at all, because he wasn't afraid of me in the first place.

It was a novel experience, and as much as I enjoyed it, I also didn't trust it.

In that moment, as I contemplated Caprice's words, I realized that this was a test. I hadn't even realized that's what I was doing, but I was testing Deacon to see what he was really made of. Most civilians couldn't handle being exposed to the criminal world.

I needed to know if he was different. If he had what it took to stand by me, or if he would end up becoming just another in a long line of casual flings.

I was snapped out of my thoughts when the hitman started laughing.

"I never thought I'd see the day. The

Wolf is getting led around on a leash by a pup. If anyone here is losing their touch, it's you. A year ago, I never would have been able to get the upper hand on you so easily. The Wolf really has lost control of his pack."

I wanted to demand that the man explain himself, but before I could, Deacon suddenly stepped forward. He had fire in his eyes and looked like he wanted to throttle the man with his bare hands, but I held him back before he could get close.

That didn't stop Deacon from running his mouth.

"You're the one who poisoned that cloth. You fucker. Nathan, let me go. I'm gonna kill him."

With one hand around Deacon's waist, I pulled him back to the far side of the room and shoved him out the door where he would be mostly out of the way.

Caprice watched the interaction with keen interest.

"How unusual. You actually let him call you by your first name. Not many are granted that privilege. Is there something special about him I'm not seeing?" With a flick of her wrist, she commanded her bodyguards. "Bring him to me. I want to get a better look at him."

The two-armed women advanced, intent on capturing Deacon.

Were they disregarding me because of my age?

Sure, I was older than them, but I was still just as lethal as I'd ever been.

It was then that I realized my preference for secrecy had circled back around to bite me. I'd overestimated Caprice even more than I thought. She not only didn't know my true name or my position as the true leader of the Chechen Mafia, but she also didn't even know my fake position. Most people within the criminal world were still aware that I was someone of importance, just not how important. Caprice didn't even know that much. To her, I was just a subordinate with a bit of power. Whenever she called me *The Wolf*, she wasn't just being snarky. She was laughing at me. From her perspective, an underling with such a grandiose moniker must seem like a joke.

She was going to regret that assumption.

Deacon still stood outside the door, clutching onto the doorframe with his attention still hyper-focused on Caprice's hitman. He didn't even seem to notice the two bodyguards stalking toward him.

I always tailored my suits specifically to fit well, but also allow ease of movement. It came in handy when I had to move quickly. Dropping down into a low crouch, I swept the legs out from under the nearest bodyguard, while pulling my gun from its holster at the same time. When I was younger, such a move would have been easy, but now my knees protested the sudden strain. It wasn't enough to throw off my balance, I didn't even stumble, but it was a reminder of the passage of time.

Someday, I wouldn't be able to fight my own fights, but today was not that day.

The bodyguard that I'd tripped rolled with her fall and quickly regained her footing, but it was just enough time for me to get a shot off at the second bodyguard. The one I shot clutched her shoulder, wounded but not dead. Before she could recover, I kicked the gun out of her hand, then dodged as the first bodyguard finally found enough balance to try and shoot me.

A bullet lodged in the wall not far from my head.

If I let myself get caught between the two of them, I'd have a difficult fight on my hands. My own gun could only fire one bullet at a time. No matter which one I shot, the other would still be able to take me out.

Who should I shoot?

Making my decision, I turned abruptly and shot Caprice. The bullet struck her low in the gut. It wasn't an immediately fatal wound, but it could take her life if she didn't get medical treatment soon.

The surprise of hearing their leader suddenly cry out in pain distracted the bodyguards just long enough for me to shoot the nearest one in the head, then turn my gun on the remaining one.

We stared each other down. Eye to eye and gun to gun. A single pull of the trigger would end it all.

"Stand down," an unexpected voice suddenly shouted.

Not daring to look away from the bodyguard still aiming their gun at me, I turned just enough to see what was going on with my peripheral vision.

Caprice's hitman stood with his arm

around Deacon's throat, and a gun at Deacon's head.

"Put your gun down, Sterling. Or I'll blow a hole through your little pet's head."

Deacon clawed at the man's arm, his nails leaving behind bright streaks of crimson. He didn't say anything, but I could tell there was a whole dictionary of curses locked behind his teeth.

Panic burned the back of my throat, but I swallowed it before it could show on my face.

"Do you take me for a fool? If I put my gun down and you'll just shoot us both." I grinned at him, letting my lip pull up into an expression that resembled a snarl and had helped earn my moniker. "You, however, are apparently a fool. You've forgotten who has the upper hand here."

A knife came flying through the air and lodged into the hitman's arm. Clutching his new wound, he was forced to drop Deacon, who immediately ran to my side.

I passed a nod of acknowledgement to the member of my own security who was standing in the door, thanking them for their assistance. My security hadn't followed me into the office, but they were still present in the building. Caprice and her people had either forgotten that little fact, or then been arrogant enough to think their own security could go toe-to-toe with mine.

In the confusion, Caprice's bodyguard grabbed her and helped her make an escape through the window. The fire escape hadn't been meant to save people from gunfire, but it still served the same purpose. The pair would live for another day.

That was fine. I hadn't truly wanted to kill Caprice anyway. I would avoid a war between our families if I could. My true target was still here, kneeling injured on the ground as his blood dripped onto the floor.

My security advanced on the injured hitman, ready to kill the man, but I ordered them to halt. Everyone in the room looked at me with confusion, but I merely turned to Deacon.

"You said you wanted to get revenge with your own hands. Well, now's your chance."

I nodded toward the gun on the floor that the hitman had dropped.

It took a moment for Deacon to realize

what I meant, but when he did, an oddly blank look came over his face. He knelt and picked up the gun with trembling hands, turning it over and over to examine it.

His hands had a unique mix of softness and strength. He had the long, graceful fingers of an artist, but they were also calloused from plenty of hard work and outdoor activity. The gun was a particularly large caliber for a handgun and was unwieldy, but it didn't look as out of place in his hands as I expected.

A moment of silence passed. No one spoke.

Then, without a hint of warning, Deacon aimed the gun and pulled the trigger.

The pop of the gunshot echoed out of the room and down the hall. The hitman stood there, stunned, as blood dripped from the new hole in his head.

Then the man collapsed, dead before he hit the floor.

Deacon stared down at the gun in his hand, trembling from head toe. It was as I feared. The reality of the situation had finally hit him, and it had hit him hard.

"Deke?" I said as I approached, though

I had no idea what to say after that. I'd barely been a teenager the first time I'd killed someone, and after so many years I barely remembered what had been going through my head at the time. I had no idea what Deacon was thinking right now.

"Sir," my security team spoke up. "We need to leave. Authorities are going to be here soon."

Grabbing Deacon by the wrist, I dragged him out of the room and into the car waiting for us in the back alley. Although he still didn't show any reaction, he also allowed himself to be easily led around.

Once inside the car, behind the safety of tinted windows, I pulled the gun out of Deacon's hand and stored it away.

"Deke. It's okay. It was self-defense. He definitely would have killed you. I... didn't think you'd actually do it. I'm sorry. I shouldn't have gotten you involved."

I'd only meant to give him a scare. Make him realize what he was asking for. I expected him to drop the gun the moment he felt its weight in his hands.

No, that was a lie. I'd challenged him because I was secretly hoping he'd pull the trigger. I wanted him to prove he had the strength to stand next to me.

And he had.

But was that success worth it?

His hands had stopped shaking, but he was still staring at them with a strange expression.

"I killed him. He poisoned Kiki, and I killed him."

He looked up at me, and I could finally see the light dancing in his eyes. Before I could question it, he grabbed my lapel and pulled me in for a kiss. His mouth molded to mine, hungrily trying to devour me whole. The unexpected passion left me speechless, and I didn't even kiss him back at first.

My lack of reaction only seemed to embolden Deacon. He climbed into my lap, heedless of the car's movement, and gripped my head with both hands to deepen the kiss even more.

Nothing could have convinced me to resist such a temptation. I slid my hands under his shirt and around his waist, holding him tightly to me and enjoying the feel of smooth, unblemished skin.

We were both panting when we finally parted.

"Deke?" I started to ask, but he cut me

off.

"Shut up." He kissed me again, this time rutting against me so I could clearly feel his arousal even through the fabric of both our pants.

With him so eager in my arms, I was quickly matching his enthusiasm, but I held back and pushed him away just enough to speak freely.

"Deke. We need to talk. This isn't... how I expected you to react."

Every muscle in his body was tense. For a moment, it looked like he might try to fight me, but then he suddenly slumped forward and buried his face against the crook of my neck.

"I know it's not normal, but I just..."

He started trembling in my arms again, but I couldn't tell if it was arousal or fear. Maybe it was both.

"I was just so angry after what happened to Kiki. And then, on the way here, I just felt so agitated. When I... When I pulled that trigger, it was thrilling. I made the bad guy go away with just the twitch of my finger. Thrilling, but also terrifying. And a relief. That guy hurt Kiki. Now, he isn't a threat anymore."

Pulling away from his hiding place

against my neck, he met my gaze, and I could see all the different emotions swimming in his eyes.

His voice took on a breathy tone, similar to the way he sounded when he was squirming in pleasure under my hands.

"And then there was you. God! The way you just took everyone out. They weren't even a threat to you. I don't know. It was just..."

He ran his mouth over the line of my jaw until he was whispering directly into my ear.

"It was really hot."

The tickle of his breath against the shell of my ear sparked desire in my veins. Maybe this was just an unhealthy reaction to the trauma of the last few days, but I didn't care. If that turned out to be the case, I would deal with it later.

A man could only be so noble when offered his desires on a silver platter.

Knocking on the window that separated us from the front of the car, I ordered the driver to take us to the nearest luxury hotel. It was New York City. There was a hotel on practically every street corner, so we didn't have to travel far. I barely had time to kiss Deacon again before the car came to a stop.

Luckily, since it was an odd time of day, the hotel lobby wasn't too busy. Renting a room only took a few minutes, but every second that passed where Deacon's skin wasn't pressed against mine felt like a small eternity.

He clung to my arm the whole time, tracing nonsensical patterns over my shoulder and chest.

At one point, when the receptionist looked away from us to focus on her computer screen, Deacon angled his hips, so the back of my hand brushed against his groin. I could feel how hard he was, and I nearly mounted him down right there on the front desk.

Everyone in the lobby knew why we were there anyway. There was only one explanation for an older man leading a younger man into a hotel, with no reservations and no luggage. Our intentions were no secret.

After an excruciatingly long wait—five whole minutes—we finally had a key to a hotel room on the top floor. This time it was Deacon who dragged me along into the elevator, and as soon as the doors closed, I pushed him up against the mirrored wall and kissed him hard enough to bruise both our lips.

At some point on our journey to the top floor, other people may have tried to get on the elevator. I vaguely remembered the doors opening more than once, but no one invaded our space and we were left alone on the elevator.

When the numbers over the door announced our floor, we parted just long enough to make our way to our room. The journey from the room's front door to the bed ended up taking nearly twenty minutes, as I kept giving in to the temptation to press Deacon against every flat surface I could find as he tugged at my clothes.

We were both wearing only our pants by the time we made it to the bed. I pressed him down on the mattress, biting and sucking at the skin of his neck. His fingers dug bruises into my shoulders as he moaned, and one of his legs wrapped around my waist.

His arousal rubbed against my own, and I didn't think twice as I slipped my hand down inside his pants to grab his ass. When I did, however, he suddenly went stiff in my arms in a way that obviously wasn't from pleasure.

I removed my hand and pulled my lips away from his neck, but he was already pulling at my shoulders, trying to drag me closer again.

"No, wait. I'm sorry. I didn't mean to react like that. It's fine. Keep going."

Looking down at him, I could see the instinctual fear in his eyes. He was more afraid now than when he'd watched me kill several people less than an hour ago.

"I'm not going to do anything you won't enjoy."

He clung to me harder. "If it's you, I'm sure I'll enjoy it. Please, Nathan. Don't leave. I need you."

"I'm not leaving," I was quick to assure him. "However... I think I have an idea."

Standing from the bed, he immediately started protesting, but I shushed him and again repeated that I wasn't leaving. Then I searched for my jacket, which had been left on the floor by the front door.

Returning to the bedroom, I pulled a pair of handcuffs out of the jacket's pocket and held them up for him to see.

Still sprawled half naked over the bed,

with his breath coming heavy and an attractive blush spreading from his cheeks all the way down to his chest, Deacon frowned at me.

"Why do you have handcuffs in your pocket?"

With a shrug, I tossed my jacket aside. "For emergencies."

Handcuffs in hand, I approached the bed.

"Do you trust me?"

CHAPTER TWELVE

Deacon

Evening light glinted off the metal handcuffs dangling from Nathan's fingers as he waited for my answer. It was said in a flirtatious way, but I knew he meant it seriously.

Did I trust him?

Any sane person would say "no". He was a member of the Mafia, and I'd just watched him kill at least one person.

Then I remembered the weight of the gun in my hand, the thrill of pulling the trigger and ending someone's life so easily.

So much more terrifying than rock

climbing.

Still lying in bed, I tried to adopt a relaxed pose. "I suppose I have to trust you. After all, you saw me kill someone."

Hearing the words leaving my mouth, I realized my true vulnerability. If Nathan wanted to ruin me, he could do so with very little effort. While I didn't understand much about the Mafia, especially not a foreign one, I knew that Nathan had been involved with things like this for a long time. He could handle it easily, and probably knew exactly how to get out of trouble. If he threw me under the bus, I would have no way to save myself.

Nathan approached the bed, moving slowly as he sat beside me. The handcuffs remained in sight at all times.

"Just because you have to trust someone, doesn't mean you do. And trust motivated by fear isn't real trust. So, think about it clearly. Do you trust me?"

Did I?

He obviously had something planned.

Could I trust him not to hurt me, even if I didn't know what he intended?

Well, if he wanted to hurt me, he would have done so by now. There was no reason to ask my permission.

Swallowing heavily, I nodded.

Nathan was obviously pleased, but he still moved as if he expected me to pull away at any moment.

"All right. Then, relax, and I promise you'll enjoy this."

It shouldn't have surprised me when he used the handcuffs to attach my wrists to the headboard.

What else were handcuffs for, after all?

Yet, I couldn't help tugging at them and testing their strength. The metal bit into my wrists a little, but not too much, since most of my weight was supported on pillows at the head of the bed.

To distract me, Nathan pressed kisses up and down my throat. He worried the sensitive skin between his teeth, no doubt leaving an impressive bruise that was going to last for days after this. It was pleasant, and instantly got my blood pumping again.

Until he started undoing my pants.

When his hand slipped inside the fabric to fondle my ass, I instinctively kicked out at him.

He must have expected this reaction because he easily caught my ankle.

"Shhh," he breathed directly into my

ear. "It'll be okay. I'm not going to do anything you won't like."

Slowly, inch by inch, he slid my pants down my legs until I was completely bare. I squirmed on the bed. His gaze on my flesh felt like the pricking of pins and needles. Oddly pleasant in the same way that poking a bruise could be addictive. It wasn't a nice feeling exactly, but I also didn't want to stop.

Nathan ran a hand down my torso, all the way from collarbone to hip. Then, he seemed to shake himself to regain control and turned his attention to removing his own pants.

This was my first time seeing him fully undressed. Until now, I'd never even seen him with his shirt off, and suddenly, I was getting an eyeful of everything at once.

His tattoos were the first thing that grabbed my attention. The snake that I'd noticed earlier wrapped around his neck wasn't alone. Several other animals adorned his skin. There was a general wolf theme, which was not surprising considering his moniker and the symbol of his home country. However, there was also a jaguar slinking around the curve of his hip, and a large bird-of-prey soaring over one pectoral. I even saw a few rabbits hiding here and there among the designs.

Along with the animals, there were also plenty of shapes and other symbols. Geometric stars scattered just below his collarbone, so specifically placed they must have depicted a constellation. Dark lines formed twisted knots around his biceps, and his forearms were covered in an odd mix of flowers and weapons.

I would have to ask him about the tattoos someday, for I was certain they all bore a special meaning. For now, I was more interested in the body that lay beneath the tattoos.

He was as well built, as I expected, though surprisingly a little thicker than his clothes made him seem. His suits were so well tailored and cut to his figure, they gave a general impression of sharpness and angles. Free of his clothes, his shoulders and chest looked broader, and his waist and thighs had more meat to them.

My hungry predator was actually quite well fed.

The thought made me laugh.

"That's not the response any man wants to get after undressing." Nathan kneeled over me, caging me in with all four of his limbs. "Care to share what's so funny?"

I only laughed harder, proving that I really lacked basic self-preservation.

"I just... I realized I'm stupid for being nervous."

"Hmmm." Nathan gave me a considering eye, like he'd expected me to say something else. "Not stupid. In fact, I'm surprised you're not more nervous. Most people would be terrified in your position."

"Well, I've always been a bit odd. Just ask anyone who's ever met me."

With a decisive nod, Nathan stood from the bed. "That is true."

"Hey!" I tried to follow him, but forgot my hands were still cuffed and ended up flopping uncomfortably to the side. "You didn't have to agree so quickly."

Despite my awkward position, I still took the time to admire his backside as he retrieved a basket off the nearby table.

After looking through the container for a moment, Nathan selected something and brought it back to the bed.

"I'm glad you're odd. We wouldn't work if you weren't."

He helped me into a more comfortable position, and it was then I noticed what he'd retrieved.

Surprised, I looked back at the basket. "Why is there a bunch of lube and stuff waiting for us here."

Nathan's grin could have given the Cheshire cat a run for its money. "The valet at the front desk will get you anything if you tip well enough."

I hadn't paid attention to what Nathan was doing when we were checking in at the front desk. I'd been too horny to care. So long as we got a room, anything would have been fine.

Apparently, Nathan had been thinking ahead.

After checking in, we'd come right up to the room. The poor valet must have booked it as fast as possible to deliver the supply basket before we got there. Plus, the fact that the hotel even had these kinds of supplies on hand meant that it wasn't the first time they'd catered to such a request. It seemed coming here hadn't been as random of a choice as I thought. The staff knew what they were doing.

The thought that Nathan may have

brought other lovers here before pricked at my brain. It would explain how he knew that the staff would be able to meet such a request. I didn't want to be jealous, but the little green-eyed monster had bitten me and wouldn't let go.

When Nathan kneeled over me again, I wrapped both legs around his waist to pull him closer.

"So, you're finally going to have your way with me?"

Nathan studied me for a moment, his gaze intense as he searched my eyes for something. I didn't know what he was looking for, but whatever he found apparently helped him make a decision. He pulled my legs from around his hips and laid them flat on the bed.

"Yes, but not like that."

Then, to my surprise, he shifted his position so he was straddling me.

My eyes felt like they were about to fall out of my head.

"Wait. What? Hold on. Are you really—" My question cut off when he leaned forward and kissed me.

The kiss didn't last long but was enough to completely steal my voice. It was as though Nathan had swallowed every word I even thought to say, because I couldn't make more than a few unintelligible sounds as he sat up straight and stared down at me.

The lid of the lube bottle made a surprisingly loud pop when he opened it. "I'm not used to doing things this way, so you'll have to bear with me. I don't think I can completely submit to you, so the handcuffs will have to stay in place. But I promise it'll be good anyway."

He couldn't be about to do what it seemed like.

It was impossible.

Yet, the impossible played out in front of my eyes as Nathan coated two of his fingers in lube, then shifted to reach around and slipped those fingers inside himself.

I couldn't have blinked even if I tried. My cock twitched and something deep in my gut twisted pleasantly as I watched Nathan preparing himself for me.

Sure, I'd had partners in the past offer to let me fuck them, but usually, I had to seek those people out specifically for such a thing. Just a convenient, lukewarm release when I was really desperate. Never from the kind of men I actually found attractive.

The men I preferred, men like Nathan who were confident and domineering, never even considered letting me top.

I shifted, trying to calm myself down as Nathan's fingers pushed a little deeper into himself. He groaned, low and guttural.

The handcuffs tugged at my wrists, reminding me of my position.

So, this is what people meant when they talked about "topping from the bottom."

I felt dizzy. I had barely taken a breath since Nathan started.

He looked down at me, face and voice both obviously strained, and gave a weak laugh. "You'd better appreciate this. I don't do this for just anyone."

Finally, after what felt like an eternity, he deemed himself prepared enough. More lube was spread over my cock as well, and the feel of his hand sliding slickly over my heated flesh nearly made me come on the spot.

Nathan's fingers pinched hard at the base of my cock, using pain to keep my orgasm at bay.

"Oh, no. I did not go through all that

trouble just for you to come that quickly. I am getting all the pleasure I can out of you."

I was panting too heavily to speak, sweat beading over my skin, so I just nodded wordlessly.

After pressing his lips to mine one more time, Nathan gripped the headboard with one hand while his other hand helped guide my desperate cock into the right position.

For someone who claimed they didn't take this position in bed very often, he certainly didn't hesitate to immediately sink down and impale himself on my shaft. We both groaned, and I dug my heels into the mattress as I fought the urge to thrust up into him.

"Fuck, you're tight."

It was, without a doubt, the best thing I'd ever felt. The heat and friction of Nathan's body was unbearably good, but what made it even better was the knowledge of *who* he was. This was a man who laughed in the face of the law and didn't hesitate to kill whoever he wanted, whenever he wanted. Other people spoke of him with fear in their voice, yet here he was, allowing me inside him in the most literal sense.

The rush of power went straight to my head, and I trembled all the way down to my toes.

The whole bed shook as Nathan gripped the headboard with both hands.

"Be good, and don't come until I say so."

Using he headboard for stability, he raised himself up until I almost slipped out of him, then dropped back down. There wasn't even time for me to moan before he did it again.

And again.

His hips and legs moved with the strength of a professional jockey as he rode me like a fucking horse. The man knew exactly what he wanted, and he was determined to take his pleasure from me.

"You... damn... liar..." I gasped as the breath was punched out of me every time he plunged back down.

The headboard creaked ominously when Nathan gripped it tighter. "How did I lie?" He paused for a breath, but never stopped the movement of his hips. "I've... given you exactly what I promised."

"You—ah... You're too good at this. You've done this before."

Nathan did stop this time, my cock buried as deep as possible inside his tight heat, obviously grinding against a particularly pleasurable spot based on the way his voice cracked.

"Didn't lie—mmm— I said I... didn't do this for *just anyone.*"

My vision flashed red, and I pulled desperately against the handcuffs.

"Who else have you let inside you?" I growled, the idea of anyone else being allowed inside him so intimately forming a lump in my gut.

I probably looked half-deranged, snarling and panting as a heated flush stained my skin.

My thrashing obviously brought Nathan even more pleasure because his arms shook as he clung to the headboard to keep himself upright.

"I see. You're a jealous little thing. Aren't you?"

Realizing I was having absolutely no effect, I slumped against the handcuffs and caught my breath.

"Not little," I grumbled without looking at him.

I felt him shift as his body squeezed tighter around my cock.

"No, you aren't."

Without warning, he started moving his hips again, bouncing even harder and faster on my cock than before. I tried to match his pace and move with him, but it was useless. Between his weight pinning me down and the handcuffs holding my arms above my head, I couldn't thrust more than an inch or two off the bed.

It didn't matter. Nathan was determined to set the pace, and he wouldn't be derailed.

Each time I watched my cock disappear inside him, the pleasure building in my gut intensified. Inch by inch, I approached the edge of climax, but I didn't want to fall until I knew Nathan was coming with me.

He'd given me an order, and I wanted to follow it.

Damn, was it hard.

My hands clawed at empty air and my toes clenched against the sheets as I tried to stave off my orgasm. Every inch of my body was alight with the need to come, and my nerves seemed to burn as I held back.

A hand stroked my cheek then trailed down the length of my neck.

"So obedient." Nathan's voice was breathless and almost inaudible over the sound of slapping flesh. "Come whenever you want. I'm almost there."

Even with permission, I held off a little longer. I wanted to see him unravel first.

It was nearly impossible. The taste of blood coated my tongue when I accidentally bit the inside of my cheek in a desperate attempt to control myself.

Yet, in the end, my efforts were worth the pain. The sight of him, back arched and hands gripping the headboard so hard both of his arms shook, was an image I would never forget. He clenched tight around me as he came, though he never stopped the movement of his hips, milking my own orgasm right out of me.

The world whited out and my voice tangled inside my throat as pleasure exploded like fireworks behind my eyes. None of my previous partners had ever come close to making me feel so good. I hadn't even known sex could be so intense, and in the back of my mind I felt cheated.

The moment lasted forever, but at the same time it was still too short. Eventually, we both sagged and collapsed against the bed. Nathan clung to the headboard just long enough to pull himself off me and slide to the side, so he didn't crush me under his weight. My hands were still cuffed, but I didn't bother to bring it up. My bones felt like liquid, and I wouldn't have been able to put my arms down even if they were released.

Lying at my side, Nathan threw one leg over me, heedless of the mess he'd left over my stomach.

"Oh, shit," I said as I looked down at the evidence of Nathan's climax painted over my skin. "We didn't use a condom. That's... that's bad, right?"

I knew better. Every gay man of the modern age knew better. Even the health classes at my uber-religious school, which had promoted abstinence as the only acceptable answer, admitted to the need for protection. While I'd never been on the receiving end of sex before, I'd fucked several one-night stands. I knew my way around a condom, but in the heat of the moment, with Nathan bearing down on me, it had completely slipped my mind.

Instead of getting upset, Nathan just laughed against my shoulder.

"Don't worry. I've checked your

medical file. I know you're clean. I am, too. I can show you mine if you need proof."

Ignoring the question of how he got my medical file in the first place, I shook my head. "No. I trust you."

I'd already trusted him with my life and my freedom. Adding my health on top of that wasn't much of a leap.

Before either of us could say anything else, we were interrupted by an unexpected banging noise coming from the other room. It sounded like wood breaking, and something metal hitting the floor. There was just enough time for Nathan to sit up on the bed before the bedroom door flew open, and we were left staring at several members of the police force.

"Step away from the bed and put your hands in the air."

Many guns pointed at us, but following their trajectory, it became obvious that they were only focused on Nathan.

Nathan reached for my handcuffs. "A least let me release him first."

When he moved toward me, the sound of several guns cocking filled the room.

"Off the bed. Now."

Raising his hands in a show of compliance, Nathan stood and stepped away from me. The guns followed him. Even naked and vulnerable, he still managed to radiate calm control, as if the police standing in our hotel bedroom had been his idea from the start.

I preferred to admire his composure, rather than think about my own position. Embarrassment burned me under the scrutiny of so many eyes. There was no denying what we had just done. While I wasn't ashamed, the remnants of my religious upbringing still insisted that sex should be a private affair, not for the eyes of others.

Not even the aftermath.

There was a commotion among the police as a familiar face pushed her way to the front of the group.

Agent Belden stood there, looking at Nathan with equal parts disgust and glee. She didn't even seem to notice me at first.

That changed when I started laughing loud enough for it to echo off the walls.

"You were right, Agent," I managed to say even as I continued to laugh, spurred on by the awkwardness of everything. "I am in handcuffs the next time we meet.

And Nathan did take care of me. You should start your own psychic hotline, because you're a God damn prophet."

Agent Belden stared at me with an odd look on her face, like she'd never been so disrespected, and didn't know how to react. The local officers, however, ignored my comments. One of them stored their gun away and approached the bed cautiously.

"Where are the keys," the officer demanded of Nathan.

Nathan didn't move, just nodded in the right direction. "There, on the side table."

A moment later, my handcuffs were removed. At first, my arms didn't want to cooperate. After being held in the same position so long, my shoulders were stiff. I gasped at the ache in my muscles as my arms collapsed against the pillows.

"Are you okay?" the officer asked as she helped me sit up.

I slapped her hand away, not in the mood to be touched by strangers, then gasped again when the bruises around my wrists made themselves known.

"Of course, I am. What kind of stupid question is that?"

Now that the shock and awkwardness

had worn off, I was pissed. My happy, post-sex afterglow had been ruined, and the sudden crash of endorphins felt like barbed wire creeping under my skin.

Rolling my shoulders to get them working again, I grabbed the nearest blanket and pulled it over my lap to preserve at least some of my dignity.

"What's this all about, anyway?"

"I would like to know that as well," Nathan spoke up from the other side of the room.

He was too far away. I hated it. We should be cuddling right now and exchanging pillow talk, not staring down the barrel of a dozen guns and twice as many judgmental eyes.

Agent Belden went back to ignoring me to face Nathan. "Don't play dumb, Sterling. You know exactly why we're here."

Still as calm as ever, Nathan bent down to retrieve his pants from the floor and started putting them on. "I assure you, I have no idea what you're talking about. If you'd care to explain, then maybe we can clear up this little misunderstanding."

Agent Belden came closer, and pulled

out a pair of her own handcuffs, nearly identical to the ones that had just held me to the bed. "We can talk all about it back at the station."

Nathan didn't say anything. Just narrowed his eyes at her as the wheels in his head turned.

I, on the other hand, started freaking out.

"Whoa. Hold on. You can't arrest him." I jumped off the bed and tripped over the tangled bed sheets.

Nathan caught me. "It's okay, Deke. You stay here while I go answer their questions. This'll all be cleared up soon. Just wait here until I come back for you."

"But—" I stared to argue, but the look in his eyes cut me off. He had a plan. I didn't know what it was, but I could see the resolution in his gaze.

I just needed to trust him.

"Fine." I made a show of crossing my arms and huffing in annoyance. "But this is not the fun weekend in New York that you promised. You owe me."

Grabbing my hand, he kissed my knuckles with the ghost of a grin on his lips. "I promise, I'll make it up to you."

I huffed again and pouted. The spoiled

brat act wasn't usually my thing, but it distracted me from the worry eating at my heart.

Nathan had a plan.

Trust him.

That mantra repeated itself over and over in my head as I watched Agent Belden handcuff him and lead him out of the hotel room.

Unfortunately, I was not left alone. Several officers stayed behind. I soon found myself moved from the bedroom to a table in the hotel room's small kitchen, thankfully dressed. Across the table sat the same officer who had uncuffed me from the bed. She seemed to be the highest rank of all the remaining officers. Her name was Officer Quinn, and she looked at me with uncomfortably sad eyes.

"It's okay," she said as she placed a hand over mine. "He's gone now."

Scowling at her, I pulled my hand out of her grip. "I'm sorry. Are you under the impression that I'm here against my will? I know the handcuffs were a bit misleading but trust me..." I leaned closer and let my smile turn just a bit lecherous. "I was a very eager participant."

The officer cleared her throat and shifted in her seat, clearly uncomfortable.

"Be that as I may, I still have a few questions for you."

Technically, since they hadn't arrested me, I didn't have to answer their questions. But I also knew that reminding them of this would only make me look suspicious.

Lounging back in my chair and crossing one leg over the other, I tossed a careless hand in the air. "Fine. Whatever. Ask away. I've got nothing to hide."

Too much?

Maybe. I'd never been interrogated before. Even when Agent Belden came to my old studio, it had been more of a threat than an interrogation.

Officer Quinn pulled out an old-fashioned notebook and pen. "You just arrived in the city today. What time was that?"

My heart thudded in my ears. This is where I could mess everything up. They'd separated Nathan and I to check if our stories lined up. If not, then it would basically be an admission of guilt. Unfortunately, I didn't know what Nathan planned to tell them. I was certain he had a plan, but there hadn't been time to "get our stories straight". If I said the wrong thing, I could accidentally end up incriminating him.

A tactic that Kiki had once taught me came to mind. The dumb blonde act had gotten her out of many tickets in the past.

I was neither blond nor female, and this was much worse than a parking ticket, but hopefully, the principle would work the same.

Resting my chin on my hand, I pretended to think for a minute. "I don't know the exact time. Nathan handled the tickets and I never looked at the clock. The sun was still up when the plane landed, though."

Not surprisingly, Officer Quinn didn't bother to write my answer down.

"I see. And what are you doing in New York? You live in Las Vegas, correct? That's a long way to fly. I'm sure you didn't come all this way just to rent a hotel room."

This one was easy. I didn't even need to feign excitement when I answered her. "We're starting a new fashion line. Well, it's not really new. It already existed, but Nathan bought the company and hired me as the lead designer to reinvent the brand's look."

I started telling her all about my design plans, and the new ideas I was eager to try. It wasn't even an act. I could go on all day about color pallets and stitching patterns if she let me. Most of the time I was holding my obsession back, so all I had to do was release the dam on my words and I wasted a significant amount of the Officer's time.

It reached the point where I was critiquing the construction of the Officer's uniform—those clothes really didn't fit her figure, and the fabric was cheap—when she finally cut me off.

"Yes, that's all very good," she said, obviously trying to hide her annoyance. "But what, specifically, are you doing here in New York? Your studio is in Las Vegas, so you must be here for some specific reason."

"Oh, I don't know," I said, waving away her question as if it were unimportant.

"You... don't know?" she repeated my answer slowly, probably wondering if she really had just heard those words.

"Yeah. Some business stuff with the company. I didn't ask. I'm a designer, not a business major. I don't bother sticking my nose in things I don't understand. Nathan just asked me to come along, so I came."

"Right." Officer Quinn's words were growing more clipped by the minute. "Why don't you walk me through what you've done today. Your plane landed. What did you do after that?"

I thought for a moment, considering many different ideas.

How did Nathan want me to reply?

Obviously, I couldn't tell her what we'd actually done, but I couldn't risk making something up that wouldn't match what he said.

I quickly ran over the timeline of our day in my head. We landed. We drove immediately to the office building where Caprice Vidales was meeting with her hitman. We killed a couple of people, including the hitman. Then we left and headed straight for a hotel to spend an unknown amount of time screwing each other's brains out.

Thinking back on it, I vaguely remembered the time on the big clock in the hotel's lobby when we checked in. Compared to the time we landed, and how long it took us to drive there, we only spent about twenty minutes at the office.

That small of a discrepancy could be explained with a minor traffic jam.

In the end, I just shrugged. "Nothing much. We landed. Then we came here."

I held back a laugh as I watched the muscles around the agent's eye start twitching. "It took you an hour to drive from the airport to the hotel?"

"What can I say? New York traffic's a bitch."

Her pen tapped against the still blank page of her notebook, leaving a little constellation of dots on the otherwise pristine surface.

"Why did you come to this hotel? There are plenty of other ones closer to the airport. We looked into it. You didn't have reservations ahead of time, so why drive all the way here?"

I looked around the hotel room as if seeing it for the first time. "I guess Nathan likes this one. I don't know. I didn't ask. As long as there's a decent bed, then its good enough for me."

I could almost hear her teeth grinding. "Mister Millar. You're not being very cooperative."

"Hmm?" I put on my best confused face. "But I answered all your questions. Is there something else you need to know?"

Her "Good Cop" act was about the crack. I could feel it. She was moments away from threatening me. The pen trembled in her hand, and her lips pulled back over her teeth like she was about to chew me to pieces.

Before she could say another word, however, the hotel room's door opened. I knew who I would see before I even turned around. Those footsteps were unmistakable.

"Nathan." Springing up from my chair, I threw myself into his arms. "You're back."

Checking the clock, I quickly realized he'd only been gone for about two hours. That was still two hours too long, but not nearly as long as I feared.

His arms wrapped tight around me. "Hello, beautiful. I told you I'd be back. Were you good while I was gone."

Grinning up at him, I nodded. "I was on my best behavior."

"Sterling?" The officer sputtered from where she still sat, staring at the both of us in wide-eyed confusion. "What? But—how?"

Nathan's hand gave my hip a squeeze as he addressed the officer. "As I said. It was a misunderstanding. Everything's cleared up now."

We obviously had a lot to talk about. He must have done something questionable to get released so quickly, but all I could feel was relief in that moment.

Turning within the circle of his arms, but never leaving his embrace, I waved at the officer with a coy twiddle of my fingers.

"Goodbye, Officer Quinn. It was pleasant talking to you."

CHAPTER THIRTEEN

Nathan

After escaping our run-in with law enforcement, Deacon and I caught the first flight back to Las Vegas. A few days later, I was sitting in my office at the *Fantaisiste* headquarters, staring out the window as my thoughts turned over and over.

I'd spent the last few days trying to figure out how Agent Belden managed to follow me to New York, and I didn't like what I'd found.

I was no amateur. I knew how to cover my tracks. The plane tickets had been booked under an alias, paid for from an account I couldn't be connected to. Plus, based on the timeframe and how quickly she'd shown up, she must have followed me to New York and rallied the local officers before I'd even committed a crime.

The only way to explain it was if she knew exactly what I had planned to do.

For the first time in a long while, I'd been put in a tough spot. On my own, I could have beaten the murder charges. I hadn't left any evidence behind for them to prove my crimes.

No security camera footage. No eyewitness willing to come forth. There hadn't even been any bodies left behind. My people had immediately disposed of them.

I was in no real danger, except for Deacon. He'd never faced a murder charge or a police interrogation before. If I'd been smarter, I would have coached him on what to say in an interrogation as soon as we left Caprice's office, but I'd been... distracted. That small mistake had nearly cost me and put him in danger.

I couldn't risk leaving Deacon in police custody longer than necessary, so I'd swallowed my pride and made a call I didn't think I would ever have to make.

I'd asked my brother for help.

He'd come through. Within half an hour of calling him, I'd been released from custody with all charges dropped. The leader of the Chechen Mafia—at least as far as the rest of the world knew—could pull a lot of strings.

Unfortunately, that meant I was going to owe my brother, and while he wasn't our family's actual leader, he was smart enough to capitalize on every opportunity.

Calling him would come back around to bite me, and it hadn't even solved the problem of Agent Belden. Just delayed her for a while. The satisfaction I felt seeing the fury on her face when I once again walked away scot-free was satisfying, but not enough to override the sense of foreboding building in my heart.

Yet, I couldn't bring myself to regret it. Deacon had done a wonderful job keeping the officers at bay until I was able to return for him. If I had any doubts about his ability to stand beside me, they had been put to rest.

The sound of Deacon's laughter drifted in from the door to the main studio where he was working. His friend had just been discharged from the hospital, so he was in particularly high spirits. If I didn't know better, it would be impossible to tell that he had killed a man just a few days ago. However, since then, I'd caught him staring off into space several times with a tangle of different thoughts turning in his eyes.

The first kill was always the hardest.

I didn't remember much from the first time I'd taken a life. It had happened so long ago. Every life I took afterward had gotten a little easier. Now, I didn't even think about it, but the first one, had caused me many sleepless nights until I'd come to terms with that new part of myself.

It must be even harder for Deacon. I'd been raised in this life from birth and knew what to expect. For Deacon, it had come out of nowhere. One day he was an ordinary citizen, and the next, he's embroiled in a criminal life.

His laughter came again, and I smiled.

As long as he kept laughing, then everything would be fine.

My phone beeped with an alert. Giving it a brief glance to confirm what it said, I left my office behind and stepped into the studio.

Kiki sat in a chair by the window, still paler than normal, but looking much better. On the floor at her feet, Deacon had spread several bolts of cloth around her like a textile rainbow. Some bolts were still whole, while others had been cut into indecipherable shapes. None of it looked like clothing, but I trusted that Deacon knew what he was doing.

After watching him for a moment, I was pulled away by a new arrival.

D'Angelo Bianchi stepped into the studio followed by his two familiar bodyguards as well as two people I didn't recognize. The bodyguards took their places by the door, while the two unfamiliar individuals stayed at D'Angelo's side.

Based on body language, I could already tell one of the unknown individuals was D'Angelo's partner. Small and slender, with cheerful eyes and artfully tousled hair. There was a burn scar on the side of his face, but his hair was styled in a way that kept it hidden, and his eyes were so bright that the scar seemed inconsequential by comparison.

The second individual was more of a mystery. Sporting a dark goth look, they were the textbook definition of androgynous, and could not be easily categorized male or female.

"D'Angelo," I greeted him. "Glad you could come on such short notice."

Under typical circumstances, two people greeting each other would generally shake hands, but we both knew better than that. D'Angelo always had at least a couple hidden weapons up his sleeve. I eyed his watch, which I knew had been fitted with a complex mechanism that shot poisoned needles. While I was on better terms with him than most other Mafia leaders, that didn't mean I was willing to trust him with my life.

D'Angelo also didn't even try to make physical contact with me. "I heard you lost one of your designers. So, I brought you some help. Oliver here is a great artist, and Ashes designs their own line of jewelry. I know neither of them is a fashion designer, but they can definitely help you out."

A replacement for the designer who'd been killed was the excuse we were using to explain his sudden trip to Las Vegas. I'd expected it to only be a cover and hadn't realized he was going to actually bring people with him.

"Did you say we've got a new designer?" Deacon called from the other side of the room.

Like a broken jack-in-the box that didn't bother waiting for the turn of a handle to pop up, Deacon stepped right into the center of our conversation and started asking Oliver and Ashes about their work.

I watched D'Angelo's eyes grow wide in surprise and prepared to intervene if necessary. However, when Oliver and Ashes both responded to Deacon's enthusiasm with equal energy, D'Angelo relaxed, so I did as well. The fond look in D'Angelo's eyes for Oliver couldn't have been more obvious. For his sake, I hoped this was a sign of trust in me. If he went around being this blatant in front of everyone, ally and enemy alike, he was going to put both himself and his lover in danger.

That was a lesson I needed to remember as well. In many ways I'd already been too obvious with Deacon, but I couldn't bring myself to regret it.

Leaving the artists to their work, I brought D'Angelo into my office.

"I assume that man, Oliver, is yours?" I said as I took my formal seat behind my desk.

D'Angelo just smirked as he helped himself to the contents of my liquor cabinet.

"And I assume that charming ball of energy is yours."

"A new prospect, but a promising one. However, that's not what we're here to talk about."

With glass in hand, D'Angelo sat himself on the other side of my desk, poised with one leg casually crossed over the other. Although I'd only known Deacon for a short time, his obsession over fashion and design had already rubbed off on me and I couldn't help but notice the quality of D'Angelo's suit.

At first glance, it seemed to be made from Italian silk, which would be apropos for the leader of an Italian Mafia family. However, after closer inspection, it turned out his suit was actually made from Russian silk. When I'd been researching what to give Deacon as a present, I'd considered Russian silk, as it was the most sought-after type of silk in the world. In the end, I'd decided it wasn't impressive enough and chosen the Vicuna fabric instead.

This train of thought led me back to my original problem. The poisoned vicuna fabric that had killed one of my designers and nearly killed Kiki. I was still trying to figure out how it was poisoned in the first place, which was why I had contacted D'Angelo.

"What do you know about pyrenic?"

Taking a sip from his drink, D'Angelo placed the glass on a small table by his chair. "Cutting right to the chase, I see. You know, when you called me, that wasn't the question I expected you to ask. Caprice has always been a pain in my ass, but she rarely uses poisons. Such options were always too... bloodless for her."

It was as I feared. Caprice must be working with someone else. It would explain why she chose such an uncharacteristic form of attack, but if her accomplice was the one who helped her get access to the Vicuna fabric I'd bought, then that meant...

D'Angelo obviously followed my train of thought, for he gave my fears a voice.

"You think there's a rat within your

own organization."

With a slow, regretful gesture, I nodded. "It would explain a few things, though it opens a lot more problems. That's why I need to know about pyrenic."

In the room beyond the door, I could just barely hear Deacon speaking with the other artists D'Angelo had brought. Their voices were so carefree. Although the two rooms were next to each other, we may as well have been in separate universes.

D'Angelo leaned back in his chair, thinking for a moment. "Pyrenic isn't a common poison. Very fast acting, but also hard to handle. Even getting just a little on your skin can have disastrous effects. Plus, it's not naturally occurring. It must be manufactured in a lab, and there's only a few places in the world capable of producing it."

The Bianchi family specialized in drugs. In the past, their business had mainly focused on recreational drugs, but in recent years, they had branched out into medical drugs.

That would, of course, also include poisons.

I gave him a pointed look, which he immediately picked up on.

"Yes, two of the labs that produce pyrenic belong to my family," D'Angelo admitted. "But whoever tried to poison you didn't get it from us."

I hadn't actually thought D'Angelo was involved in the poisoning attempt, but it was good to hear it from the man's mouth.

"I need a list of all the labs capable of producing this poison."

D'Angelo didn't say anything as he took a long sip of his drink.

The cheeky bastard.

If I hadn't already expected such a response, I would have been annoyed.

"In exchange, I'll owe you another favor."

With a smug grin, D'Angelo set his drink back down, now almost completely empty. "Seeing as how you were doing me a favor in the first place, it feels like we've come full circle."

"If it reveals a traitor among my people, I'll consider this whole thing worthwhile."

"Actually," D'Angelo sat up quickly, his eyes glinting with a sudden idea. "I'm going to capitalize on that favor right now. Oliver's friend who came with us. Ashes. I need you to hire them fulltime."

"Sure," I instantly agreed. "But why. That seems like a strange request. Is there something unusual about them?"

"They're not involved with any criminal business, although they are aware of things. The problem is that they live in a run-down little shack of a workshop that isn't nearly safe enough for Oliver to spend time in. But I don't want to separate him from his friend. If you hire Ashes for me, then I know Oliver's friend is in a safe place and I won't have to worry about him every time he wants to visit."

I didn't want to admit it, but for a moment, jealousy pricked at me like an acupuncturist's needle, painful but also therapeutic.

D'Angelo obviously cared deeply for Oliver. So much so, he was willing to call in a favor just to secure his lover's friend. I realized I wanted that kind of relationship with Deacon. The two of us had great sexual chemistry, and I definitely liked him. It even seemed like he would be a good fit with the less "clean" aspects of my life.

But would I be willing to sacrifice for him?

Or even sacrifice for his friend just because it would make him happy?

That, I couldn't say for sure.

Once D'Angelo and I were in agreement, we went back to the studio where our little group of artists were working. They'd also been busy. Cloth was everywhere, and they were gathered around a table spread with dozens of drawings.

Neither D'Angelo nor I had the heart to interrupt their creative fervor, and just stood to the side watching them.

If there really was a traitor within my own organization, things were likely going to get worse before they got better. An insider could do a lot more damage than most enemies.

They might also know how important Deacon was becoming to me. I may as well have painted a target on his back.

I'd do what I could to keep him safe, but even I couldn't be everywhere at once.

I needed to make sure Deacon knew how to defend himself.

CHAPTER FOURTEEN

Nathan

"Why are we here again?" Deacon asked as I led him inside the concrete building. It didn't look like anything noteworthy on the outside and was the least glamorous property I owned. I'd bought the indoor shooting range a few years ago for one reason, and one reason only. So I could have the place all to myself whenever I wanted, no question asked.

"The other day, when we faced Caprice and her hitman, that was the first time you'd ever held a gun, wasn't it."

For a moment, I worried that reminding him of the incident might bring up some latent trauma, but Deacon just smiled up at me.

"Pretty good for my first time, right? I got 'em in one shot."

Shaking my head with a fond expression, I wiped the grin off his face by pinching his ass. He yelped and pouted at me, but I was glad to see he no longer acted defensively to such attention as he had in the past.

"It's a miracle you managed to hit anything when you were holding the gun all wrong. Now, I'm going to teach you how to shoot properly, so next time you don't have to rely so much on luck."

The shooting range was completely empty. A dozen dividers marked out each shooting station, with various targets set up at the far end of a long, reinforced corridor. One of the shooting stations had already been outfitted with a selection of weapons, as I'd requested.

My security remained outside the door, keeping the building under watch, so Deacon and I were completely alone within the cold gray environment.

Somehow, despite the complete lack of ambiance, when Deacon eagerly pulled me over to the shooting station, it felt as cozy and intimate as my own bedroom.

"Look at all this," Deacon gushed, running his fingers delicately over the various weapons without picking them up. "Do I really need to know how to use all of these? I mean, it's awesome, but some of this..." He tapped the handle of an AR-57 submachine gun. "Seems like overkill."

I picked up the submachine gun, turning it over in my hands to inspect it. The thing was brand new. Metal burrs still curled around the edges of the spot where the serial number had been shaved off.

"Hopefully, you'll never need to use something like this, but I'll rest much more soundly at night knowing that you can if you have to." Putting the submachine gun down, I picked up a Remington pistol instead. "However, we'll start with something smaller."

"What?" Deacon pressed himself against my side, so the heat of his body chased off the chill of the air-conditioning. "You think I can't handle such a large weapon."

Gripping his chin with one hand, I pressed a quick kiss to his lips. "I think you can manage anything you get your hands on." As I stared into his slightly dazed eyes, I wrapped his fingers around the handle of the pistol. "But let's start with this."

We started with how to load the weapon and went over the basics of gun safety. The last thing I wanted was for him to accidentally injure himself when I was trying to make him safer.

Once it was loaded, I stood behind him at the shooting station and showed him how to hold the gun and aim.

Deacon paid careful attention the whole time, but also pressed himself back against me so his ass lined up right with my groin.

It wasn't the first time I'd shot a gun while hard. Once, many years ago, an assassin attacked me while I was in a hotel room with a hired companion. That time, I'd been hard and naked, but still managed to kill my assailant without getting a scratch.

This was much more pleasant.

With my hands wrapped around his, I guided Deacon through the process of aiming the gun. Then, with a squeeze of the trigger, the weapon fired. It didn't hit the bullseye, but we at least managed to leave a hole in the paper target.

Deacon hummed with pleasure as he looked back at me over his shoulder. "Even something so small can have a kick."

Unable to help myself, I pulled his hips against me and teased several love bites into his neck.

"Any bullet will work if it hits the right spot."

He tipped his head to the side, silently begging for more of my attention.

I gave him one more kiss, then placed the gun back into his hand.

"So, let's practice your aim some more."

It took several clips of ammunition, but eventually Deacon was able to land a hit inside the bullseye with minimal help from me. Once he was comfortable with the Remington pistol, we moved onto others. We briefly experimented with everything, including handguns, revolvers, single-actions, bolt-actions, and even shotguns and assault rifles.

Most of the weapons were practical things that Deacon might possibly encounter if he continued to stand at my side.

There was one weapon on the table, however, I was almost certain he would never encounter. Even if he did end up in a firefight with such a gun, it would only be from a distance.

The Dragunov sniper rifle required a tripod to hold it up on the table. The extra extension on the end of the barrel would have made it look unbalanced if it weren't for the mounted sight scope that rivaled the size of a telescope lens.

"You'll have to bend over for this one," I whispered directly into Deacon's ear. The effect was probably ruined by the earplugs he was wearing to protect his hearing, but a blush still spread down his neck.

I showed him how to bend down and align the butt of the gun with his shoulders and place his eye against the scope. Once he was in position, I could have stepped back, but it was so much better to plant my feet a little wider and stand directly behind him.

If anyone asked, I was just trying to give him extra stability to brace against.

Deacon only pulled the trigger once. The rifle made little sound, but it kicked hard enough to push him back against me.

"Ow," he groaned and rubbed his shoulder. "That's going to leave a bruise. How does anyone fire something like this more than once."

When the gun jolted him backward, his hips pushed directly against my already eager arousal. I breathed deeply as sparks of pleasure danced up my spine, then leaned down to place my hands on the table to either side of Deacon's waist.

"You'd get used to it with practice. Although—" I gasped when Deacon wiggled his hips. "A true expert can get the job done with one shot."

Deacon moaned as I started grinding against him and his head dropped onto the table. His fingers still clung to the girth of the large gun, so just to be safe, I put the safety on and removed the bullets.

His legs spread to give me more space to press closer. Half bent over him, I ran a hand up and down his back while I reached around to unbutton his fly with my other hand.

As soon as his zipper came down, he grabbed my hand.

"I don't—" He gasped in arousal and thunked his forehead against the table. "I want to. But I don't know if I can."

Enfolding his hand within my own, I formed his fingers into a fist and rapped his knuckles against the table.

"If you want to stop, just knock like this. We'll stop immediately."

He looked at me over his shoulder with lust-filled eyes. He thought about it for a moment, then nodded, and wriggled his hips again in invitation.

I slipped one hand down the front of his pants and found him just as hard as I was. Possibly even more. With a light, delicate touch, I stroked him until I heard him panting. Then, with the hand not inside his pants, I pushed two fingers past his lips and into his mouth.

He knew exactly what I wanted him to do and started sucking on the digits.

I toyed with his tongue, getting my fingers as wet as possible. His whimpers vibrated against my fingertips, urging me on without a word.

Once I deemed it enough, I pulled my fingers from his mouth and slipped that hand down the back of his pants. Using his own spit as lube, I rubbed between the cleft of his ass and circled around his hole. His whole body trembled, but he didn't try to push me away or knock against the table to signal for me to stop.

Slowly, always looking for any sign of discomfort, I pressed one finger inside him, breaching that virgin ring of muscles for the first time. Based on Deacon's stories of his past exploits, it was the only part of him that hadn't been touched. While I didn't care about his previous experiences, virginity had never mattered to me much, I was proud to claim this one part of him.

He was incredibly tight, and one finger barely managed to fit. I could tell from the sound of his voice that he was uncomfortable even though my finger was only halfway in. My other hand sped up on his cock, trying to draw his attention away from the intrusion and replace discomfort with pleasure.

It seemed to work. His moans turned soft and breathless once again, and he even pushed his hips back against me, forcing my finger deeper all on his own.

Once I was inside him up to the last knuckle, I curled my finger and started searching for the one spot I knew would make everything better.

Usually, for someone's first time, it took a little finding, but Deacon's body seemed eager for pleasure. I found the correct spot almost immediately. As soon as I touched that sensitive gland, his whole back arched and he cried out.

"What?" he gasped as he clawed at the table and clung to the rifle that he was still laying half-sprawled across. "That's what it feels like? Fuck!"

Any further words were cut off when I started thrusting my finger in and out of him, making sure to hit that sweet spot every time. Soon, his inexperienced muscles loosened up enough to allow for a smooth slide, and I added a second finger inside him.

He let out a high-pitched moan, then silenced himself by biting his own arm.

My hand on his cock stopped. Removing it out of the confines of his pants, I grabbed his hair and pulled his head away from his arm.

"Oh, no. Don't silence yourself. There's no one here but me to hear you, and I want all of your noises."

He whimpered and nodded as best he could with my hand tangled in his hair.

His lips were bitten red and glistened with spit from his panting.

I kissed him deeply, pushing my tongue into his mouth at the same time I started thrusting my fingers inside him faster. His desperation tasted so sweet that I didn't want to let him go, but I had more plans for him.

Breaking the kiss and releasing his hair, I slid my hand back into the front of his pants to take his cock into my grip once again.

I timed the movement of my hands, stroking his cock at the same pace as I fingered him. The pleasure must have bombarded him from both sides, and I could feel him quickly approaching his climax. Every muscle in his body seized, and his feet actually left the floor to flail wildly, leaving all his weight resting on the table.

Both of my hands sped up, pushing him harder and faster to draw out his orgasm as long as possible. He was openly sobbing by the time it ended, his spend spilling over my fist to coat the inside of his underwear, but there was obvious delight dancing in his eyes.

I removed my hands from him but

didn't step away as I let him catch his breath. He seemed so worn out, I expected him to remain draped boneless over the table for some time. However, he surprised me by immediately planting his feet on the floor and standing. Turning in my arms to face me, he wrapped his arms around my neck and pulled me into a hungry kiss.

I'd barely started to reciprocate before he pulled away and looked at me with a smirk.

"My turn."

Before I could ask him what he meant, he dropped to his knees and pawed at my fly.

There was just enough time for me to grab the edge of the table with both hands before he succeeded in his quest. With the confidence of a professional, he pulled my cock free and swallowed it down.

Deacon hadn't been lying when he claimed to be very experienced with this aspect of sex. He didn't gag at all as he took me deep enough to hit the back of his throat, and his tongue moved with such agility that it seemed twice as long as it actually was.

In just a few moments, I was grasping

the table so tightly that my knuckles cracked. I was torn between two different desires. Part of me wanted to throw my head back and close my eyes to fully focus on the pleasure assaulting my body, while another part of me wanted to keep my eyes open to watch every movement of Deacon's head bobbing between my legs.

I finished embarrassingly quickly. The warmth of his mouth mixed with the squeeze of his throat was pure heaven, and the dexterity of his lips and tongue caused my blood to boil in my veins. In less than a minute, my orgasm ripped through me with a violent force and I erupted in his throat, Deacon humming his appreciation as he happily took all that I had to give him.

I'd been shot with bullets that packed less punch.

Deacon stood from the cold floor with a smug grin on his lips, but he didn't stay smiling for long. As soon as he was off his knees, I pressed him back against the table and claimed his mouth for my own, uncaring of the taste of myself on his tongue.

There was no contest. Every other partner I'd ever had was officially wiped from my mind. Even if Deacon and I could never do more than this, I would be satisfied, but based on today's experience, I had hope that we would be able to take that final step very soon.

CHAPTER FIFTEEN

Deacon

It had only been a few months since my last fashion showcase, yet I was more nervous now than I had been before. This was my first event as the *Fantaisiste* lead designer. It had to be perfect. So far, everything was going smoothly. No dead models turned up in the closets. Yet, my heart still pounded in my chest as the clock counted down.

"Hey," Oliver said from where he was standing next to me in the prep room. "You okay? Your hands are shaking."

Looking down, I realized he was right.

Fuck.

My hands were shaking.

There was no room for pockets on my skin-tight pants—which had been Kiki's choice—so I crossed my arms and clenched my hands into fists.

"Yeah, it's just nerve-wracking, you know? Everyone's going to be looking at my work. What if they hate it? Nathan put all this together. What if he hates it?"

The prep room was large to accommodate all the models and staff, but most of the space was taken up by workstations. There were dozens of people clustered into the room, getting models into outfits, applying makeup, and styling hair. I was so used to doing all the work myself. Having an actual crew to handle the brunt of it was a foreign concept. Luckily, Kiki was perfectly happy to take over the job of manager and delegate tasks.

That left me standing uselessly in the corner, though, not sure what to do with myself. Oliver and Ashes joined me in my vigil. I'd asked Nathan about the nature of his work with D'Angelo only once and had been given a vague enough answer to make it clear that D'Angelo was also tied up with the mafia, and I didn't want to know more than that. Oliver and Ashes were aware of things, and it was surprisingly helpful to have someone to talk to who understood my perspective. Suddenly being dropped into a world of criminal activity wasn't an easy adjustment. I hadn't even told Kiki about the true nature of our employment with *Fantaisiste,* and that secret weighed heavily on me.

I'd have to tell her eventually.

Maybe after the show.

For now, it was just good to have someone to talk to that I didn't need to hide the truth from.

Something came flying toward me, and I caught it just in time to keep it from smacking me in the face.

"What the hell?"

The thing I'd caught turned out to be a fidget spinner.

From the couch where they were lounging, Ashes grinned at me. "Use it to keep your hands busy. It always helps when I'm nervous."

Oliver smacked his friend's feet, forcing them to move so he could sit on the couch as well. "Since when are you ever nervous?"

Ashes stuck their tongue out at Oliver, which also showed off the barbell piercing that usually remained hidden behind their teeth. "Hey. I get nervous. I just don't show it. That's how you know the fidget spinner works."

Although they hadn't told me much about themselves, it was obvious that Oliver and Ashes were old friends. They reminded me of Kiki and myself in many ways. Neither of them were fashion designers, so I had been unsure how much help they would actually be. However, Oliver's artistic eye and Ashes's sense for aesthetic construction really helped get the whole project together. We'd finished the collection with a few days to spare, and I had to admit the designs were some of my best ever.

Ashes had made pieces of custom jewelry that matched perfectly to each outfit, and though they could be worn separately, it all fit so flawlessly together that the jewelry seemed like part of the clothing. The ensembles were stunning, in my opinion. I just hoped everyone else thought so, too.

Oliver had such a deft hand with a pencil and paper, I could describe some vague idea in my mind, and he would immediately sketch it to life. The collection definitely wouldn't have been the same without both of them.

I was glad when I heard that Nathan had agreed to hire Ashes permanently, and wondered if we could bring Oliver on as well. They were both great artists on their own but worked best as a team. Although, I was pretty sure that D'Angelo and Oliver were an item, so that might not be possible.

Maybe I could hire Oliver as a freelance artist to work remotely.

Eventually, with less than an hour before the show, Kiki announced that everything was ready and all they needed was my final inspection. The models were lined up in the order they would appear in the show. I walked down the line, inspecting each one carefully, and made a few minor adjustments. One model's belt wasn't tied the right way, so it sat on her hips at an angle that didn't align with the seams of the clothing, and another was wearing the wrong pair of earrings.

Overall, however, it was perfect.

Surely, Nathan was going to love it, and it was going to blow all our competition out of the water.

After what that woman, Caprice Vidales, had done to Kiki and tried to do to Nathan, I wanted to hit her where it would hurt.

Her bank account.

I'd learned that, for those raised in the Mafia, life was cheap. People like Caprice and Nathan were so used to death threats and murder, physical pain meant nothing. Even if they were killed, they would just see it as a failed business transaction. I didn't blame them for that kind of skewed attitude. That was the world they lived in. Being too sensitive to death and danger would just get them killed faster.

Money, however, was a powerful motivator. The more money I could take from Caprice by stealing her business, the better.

It was almost time for the show. The models were ready. There was nothing left for me to do.

The prep room led to a makeshift backstage area. It almost looked like a traditional backstage, but when I looked up, I could see the open blue sky.

Rather than arrange the event at a

traditional venue, Nathan had decided to do something a little different.

Well, not so little.

More like, a lot different.

Nathan claimed he wanted my work to be seen by as many people as possible. When I snuck a look through the curtain out toward the runway that waited for us, my eyes widened.

Nathan was certainly going to get his wish.

The fidget spinner twirled like a propeller between my clammy fingers in an effort to keep me calm. I could practically feel the wind coming off the little toy, it was moving so fast.

I had no idea how, but Nathan had managed to rent out the fountain in front of the Bellagio hotel. It was an iconic Las Vegas landmark, visited by thousands of tourists every day.

A glass bridge had been erected over the pool practically overnight, which would act as the runway for the models. It was far enough away from the water jets to keep the outfits from getting wet, which had been my biggest concern when Nathan proposed the idea.

Already, hundreds of people were

gathered around the area, curious about what was going on. A special seating area had been arranged for high-profile guests, but the overall size of the audience could have rivaled one of Thierry Mugler's shows.

When the time to start the show finally arrived, an announcer stepped out onto the bridge with a microphone in hand. The clear material of the bridge made it look like he was walking on water, and I could already imagine what the models would look like when they stepped out onto the ethereal stage.

"Welcome," the announcer said, his voice projecting from hidden speakers so everyone could hear him. "To this unique show held right here on the streets of Vegas. *Fantaisiste* is excited to announce its new look with a brand-new fashion line, inspired by the very city of Las Vegas itself."

I wasn't sure if it was Nathan or Kiki who had hired the announcer, but they'd made a good choice. The announcer hyped up the show with so much authentic energy and enthusiasm, it seemed like we were about to witness a pivotal moment in history.

When the announcer finished, the first model stepped out among a roar of clapping hands from the audience and splashing water from the fountain.

Unlike most fashion runways, where the models would walk to the end, do a few turns, and then walk back, the bridge had no turnaround spot. Instead, the models had been instructed to pause at the center of the bridge in order to show off the outfit. I'd specifically chosen models with backgrounds in dance. Rather than just standing straight, I wanted them to really show off each outfit's movements.

The first model wore a long, flowing skirt with several layers inspired by the colors of a desert sunset and the feeling of wind in my hair as I stood at the top of a tall cliff. The model twirled and dipped in a series of ballet inspired moves that brought the skirt to life, and her jewelry sparkled in the afternoon sun.

The audience's applause grew louder when she finished, barely even listening to the announcer explaining the inspiration for the outfit. After giving a quick bow, the model walked off the other side of the bridge, making way for the next one in the lineup.

This model was male, and his outfit had a more urban feel meant to represent the structure of the city. However, instead of using graphic prints with many colors, I'd chosen a monochrome palette of black and gold. Night was when the city of Las Vegas really shone, and no one could deny the splendor of its glittering lights.

Like the previous model, this one also stopped at the center of the bridge for their moment in the spotlight. Instead of ballet, the model performed a few gravity defying hip-hop maneuvers that really tested the outfit's range of movement. When the model dropped into a backspin, I was delighted to discover an effect I hadn't predicted. The model's quick spinning caused the black and gold colors of his outfit to blur together, giving a momentary impression of tiger stripes.

It wasn't planned, but I loved it, and I joined in with the audience's applause from my place backstage.

The show continued in this way, one model after the other, each getting their moment to show off. One of my favorite outfits came in the very middle, made entirely from neon fabric and accessories.

Getting it to light up while still being wearable had been a nightmare, but worth it. The model moved without any hindrance, and her glowing clothes left streaks of afterimage color, like she was painting the air with each wave of an arm or leg.

The audience's applause died down in the lull between models, but it never really stopped. They were obviously enjoying the show as much as I was. What most people didn't realize, however, was that every piece I'd designed was a direct comparison to an outfit from *Minestra,* Caprice Vidales's fashion line. The comparison wasn't too apparent since I'd put my own artistic spin on everything. I didn't want to be accused of plagiarism, after all.

Or even worse, labeled as "unoriginal".

The comparison was subtle, obvious only if one knew to look for it. I'd worked hard to make sure that anything *Minestra* was known for, *Fantaisiste* would now be known for instead.

Only better.

The last piece of the show, the grand finale, wouldn't make sense to anyone who didn't know Las Vegas's history, but it looked stunning, nonetheless. The model was draped in an oversized coat made entirely out of pastels and light green fabric. She looked like a spring goddess that had decided to walk among mortals.

Unlike the other models, she didn't dance when she reached the center of the bridge. In fact, she barely moved at all.

After the expectations left by the previous displays, the audience fell silent as they waited to see what would happen.

When she was sure she had everyone's attention, the model flipped her coat off her shoulders, so it turned inside out, revealing that it was actually a second dress. The new dress slid down around her, covering the soft pastel colors of the first dress with a new design of sharp metallics.

The model turned like a queen, graciously allowing the audience to gaze upon her altered appearance. As she moved, the metallic fabric occasionally parted enough to flash hints of the pastel colors beneath.

Absolutely stunning.

I held my breath, feeling giddly as an electric rush of pride raced though my veins, and truly prayed Nathan liked the unique piece as much as I did.

The name Las Vegas translated to "The Meadows" because the city was meant to become a green oasis in the middle of the desert. This never happened, due to the obvious lack of water, but the city persisted anyway.

This was one of the things I liked about the city. It thrived on defying expectations and not being what it was supposed to be.

Although, now that I thought about it, there was a deeply rooted link between the Mafia and Las Vegas as well. The criminal underworld played a big part in shaping "Sin City" into the desert jewel it was today.

It seemed I shared more in common with this city than I even realized.

When the last model successfully completed her walk and stepped off the bridge, I let out my held breath in a rush. Oliver and Ashes each gave me a high-five.

"Yeah! Even better than I expected," Ashes cheered.

"It was good," Oliver agreed. "Although, I think one of the models may have broken a shoe on their way off the bridge. Her last few steps were a bit unbalanced. I hope they get it fixed in time for the encore walk."

Just as the words left Oliver's mouth, all the models appeared again, this time coming from the other side of the bridge in single file line to show off the whole collection together one last time. Just as Oliver had said, one of the models had definitely broken a shoe. It looked to have been hurriedly reattached to her foot with straps that were similar but not quite the same material as the original shoe.

One of Kiki's sharp manicured nails suddenly poked me right under my ribs. "What are you just standing there for? Get ready. It's time for your speech."

Oh, right.

The speech.

I'd been so focused on each outfit that I'd almost forgotten my role in the show.

Tugging at my clothing to make sure everything was in place, I stepped out onto the bridge. The glass under my feet had been carved with a subtle texture to make walking on it easier, but I still feared I would slip and plunge into the fountain. Watching my feet only made it worse, since I could see right through the bridge to the water below.

The models had danced on this thing?

Whatever we were paying them, we needed to double it.

I'd already been fitted with a microphone backstage, so my voice rang out through the speakers as I recited the speech Kiki had written for me. My mind was completely blank as I looked out over the audience filling the sidewalk and spilling onto the street, which had, thankfully, been shut down before the show. I couldn't remember a word of what I was supposed to say, but my mouth went through the motions anyway, guided only by muscle memory after Kiki had made me practice the speech so many times.

Smart woman.

It was a generic composition, thanking everyone who had helped me, and waxing a bit of poetic about the freedom and beauty of Las Vegas that inspired me. Then, of course, I ended it by thanking everyone who had enjoyed the show, claiming that their satisfaction made all of my efforts worthwhile.

That was a lie, truth be told. I only

cared about one person's opinion. So long as Nathan liked it, the rest of the audience could hate every outfit I put on the runway, and I wouldn't bat an eye.

Still, the public were the ones who would buy *Fantaisiste's* products, so they were the ones I needed to keep happy at that moment.

I finished my speech and gave a dramatic bow. With the afternoon sun beating down on the back of my neck, I was glad for Kiki's choice of clothes for me. The tight pants were hot, but the shirt compensated for the temperature and gave my skin room to breathe. Missing sleeves, and the front mostly open, it was meant to look like a "deconstructed" suit. A homage to the "deconstructed" kimono that had started everything. Most people wouldn't get the reference, but I didn't care.

It made me smile and felt like my own little secret hidden right under everyone's noses.

When I stepped off the bridge and into the shade of the backstage area, I stumbled as the weight of relief hit me.

The show was over.

I'd done it, and based on the sound of

the audience's applause, it had been a success.

A strong hand caught me under the arm and held me upright.

Looking up, I met Nathan's gaze. As usual, his expression gave nothing away.

Was he happy?

Angry?

Disappointed?

Tugging nervously at my clothing again, I stared at his chin rather than meet his eyes.

"So... How was it? Did you like it?"

My hands were restless and wouldn't stay still.

Where had I put that fidget spinner?

I could use it now.

Nathan studied me for a moment, never letting go of my arm even as his expression remained frustratingly neutral.

"What do you think?"

Biting my lip, my gaze dropped down a few inches to look at the tattoo on his neck that peeked out from the collar of his shirt.

"Well, I certainly hope you liked it. I mean, logically, you should. You've seen all the outfits before. Nothing should be a surprise. But seeing something in the workshop isn't always the same as seeing everything together on the runway."

I was rambling. I knew this, but I couldn't seem to stop. My words kept coming, making less and less sense, until the feeling of Nathan's strong finger under my chin brought my word vomit tirade to an abrupt halt.

He tipped my head up, so I was looking directly into his eyes. For a moment, his expression was so intense it made me squirm, but then a small smile turned up the corners of his mouth.

"I loved it. It was... fantastic."

Overcome with excitement, I jumped onto him and wrapped my arms around his neck in a tight hug. He didn't even stumble, slipping his arms underneath my ass as he was suddenly burdened with my weight, and holding me close, so my feet dangled off the floor.

No words were needed. Every feeling coursing through me was expressed when I pressed my mouth to his, and he didn't hesitate to kiss back.

CHAPTER SIXTEEN

Deacon

After-parties were not my favorite thing. Not my least favorite thing. That honorable title would always belong to cockroaches.

Seriously, fuck cockroaches.

They gave me goosebumps just thinking about them.

So, not as bad as cockroaches, but still not my favorite thing.

I was wiped out after putting in so much work to get the show together. Now that it was done, just wanted to go home and enjoy a long bubble bath to unwind. Instead, I was stuck socializing with a bunch of rich assholes simply because they were the "elite" of the fashion world, and I needed to impress them.

Although, an after-party was where I met Nathan, so maybe they weren't so bad.

Remembering our fateful first encounter, I clung tight to my glass of champagne to avoid repeating history and took a long drink.

Luckily, Nathan and Kiki were happy to do most of the talking as we mingled among the crowd. A few people asked me about my designs and my artistic style, but I didn't usually get more than a sentence or two out before they moved onto the next topic.

The only people who cared about the artistic process were other designers, and there were very few of those here.

They were all probably home, working on their next creation and relaxing in bubble baths, just like I would rather be.

The Bellagio's Grand Ballroom could hold over four thousand people. So, although Nathan had invited enough guests to throw a lively after-party, it still wasn't enough to fill the room to capacity. There was plenty of space for everyone. I had no excuse to feel claustrophobic, yet I did. Most of the time I stayed near either Kiki or Nathan, happy to let them lead the conversation and filling in my opinions only when asked.

That way, everything went smoothly, and my impulsive tongue didn't get me in trouble.

At least Oliver and Ashes were there, accompanying D'Angelo. Whenever the social niceties and fake smiles got to be too much, I could step aside to discuss the show with them.

They'd noticed the unintended tiger stripe pattern on the second model as well, and we gushed about it together. Plus, I couldn't seem to stop complimenting Ashes's jewelry, which looked even better in the noonday sunlight than I'd hoped. We also nitpicked the flaws, such as one model's broken shoe, and the rosette that had fallen off my finale piece right before the show started, which I had been forced to cast aside.

Even the flaws were fun to discuss. Only someone with an artist's eye would notice such a small detail, like a single missing flower, or care enough to bring it up. Unfortunately, I couldn't spend the entire night talking with them, and had to get back to the "important" people.

I made my way through the room, smiling and shaking hands with everyone who greeted me, and even stopped to take pictures with a few of the more eager guests. Eventually, I managed to make my way back to Nathan's side. He was speaking with some investors, using a bunch of terms and words I barely understood. The way they spoke made it seem like money was a living thing with a mind of its own that had to be tricked and coaxed into their bank accounts.

They sounded more like hunters stalking prey rather than businessmen.

These were the worst kinds of conversations. The ones I couldn't even participate in, and my smile felt hollow as I nodded along like I knew what they were talking about. Nathan must have sensed my discomfort and draped a reassuring arm over my shoulder without even a pause in his conversation. A few of the investors eyed his arm around me with obvious disgust but said nothing. It was the twenty-first century, and homosexuality was still not universally accepted. Yet, enough money could persuade even the most outspoken bigots to keep their mouths shut.

Eventually, the conversation ended, and the investors walked away. Nathan took the opportunity to lean over and press a quick kiss to my cheek and whisper directly into my ear. "You doing okay?"

"Yeah." I sighed. "Just tired. It's been a long day."

He hummed in agreement and his breath tickled my ear. A flush of arousal ran through my veins right to my dick, and I desperately tried not to squirm.

Of course, Nathan noticed immediately and laughed at me under his breath.

"Not too tired, it seems."

"Shut up," I hissed at him between my teeth. "This is your fault. You always talk right into my ear like that during sex, so of course I'm going to respond." I batted at my ear, as if that would cleanse the arousal that was already thrumming under my skin, but it did nothing.

After a quick squeeze to my shoulders, Nathan let me go. At first, it seemed like he was about to walk away and leave me to deal with my problem on my own, but then he grabbed my wrists and dragged me with him.

Not that I needed to be dragged.

Sometimes I felt like a well-trained dog. All he had to do was tell me to heel and I would follow him like a circus poodle.

I even discreetly wiped my mouth with my free hand just to make sure I wasn't panting.

The bathrooms in the Bellagio were exactly what one would expect of a hotel of such high caliber. Fancy, large, and most importantly, clean. However, as Nathan pressed me up against the sinks and kissed me until my legs gave out, I wouldn't have cared if it was a truck stop toilet, so long as he kept touching me.

The bathroom also wasn't empty. A moment after we arrived, a stranger stepped out of one the cubicles, only to freeze at the sight of us. The man quickly apologized and left without washing his hands.

"We're going to get kicked out for indecent exposure," I said between kisses.

Nathan just grunted and lowered his head to run his lips along my neck. I wasn't foolish enough to think he hadn't noticed the stranger. He was too careful to be so oblivious. No, he'd simply deemed the stranger a non-threat and proceeded to ignore them.

Voyeurism really wasn't one of my kinks, so how did I keep ending up having sex with Nathan in public places?

Furthermore, how come I kept enjoying it?

Lifting me to sit on the fancy marble sink, Nathan guided my legs to wrap around his hips. The downside to wearing such tight pants was that they took forever to take on and off, so Nathan didn't even try. He seemed content to keep worshiping my neck and sucking bruises into my skin while grinding against me.

I growled low in frustration and fumbled for the button to my fly. My pants were quickly growing too tight. Maybe I wouldn't be able to remove them, but I could at least give myself some relief.

It took some struggling, and Nathan had to stop and help me, but in the end, I got my pants undone enough to free my suffering cock from its prison.

Almost as soon as I felt blessedly cool

air on my heated skin, Nathan wrapped his hand around my shaft and started stroking me.

Moaning, I let my head fall back and knocked it against the mirror over the sink.

"Ah, fuck, these pants were a bad idea."

"But you look so good in them," Nathan said directly into my ear. The rumble of his voice sent another wave of arousal rushing though me, and I bit the inside of my cheek to keep myself from coming on the spot.

Yep, that Pavlovian response was deeply ingrained and wasn't going away any time soon. I'd just have to accept my fate and a future of inconvenient boners whenever I felt the vibration of his voice.

I knew ears could be an erogenous zone. I just never expected it to be true for me. Things had been so much easier when all my sensitive spots resided under my clothes.

With only a few strokes of my cock, Nathan already had me on the edge of orgasm, but he made sure to never let me finish. He kept his strokes just a little too light.

My fist hammered against the sink under me in frustration. "Damn it, Nathan. Stop teasing me."

His only response was to smirk at me before biting harder at my neck.

I moaned again as he twisted his wrist in a way that nearly sent me over the edge, then kicked my feet uselessly in the air when it still wasn't enough for me to finish.

Mustering as much composure as I could, I glared at him, then reached for the zipper of his fly as well. Nathan's own arousal sprang free with just as much enthusiasm as my own. Yet, before I could get my hands on him, he grabbed both my wrists and pinned them above my head against the mirror.

"So disobedient. You can't just let me have my fun, can you?"

I squirmed, trying and failing to free myself.

"Nathan, please," I whined. "You're killing me."

Keeping my wrists pinned with one hand, he wrapped his other hand around both our cocks at once.

"Not yet, I'm not."

He stroked our cocks at the same time

so both shafts were engulfed in the heat of his palm. The friction of his calloused hand juxtaposed against the velvet slide of his arousal made me shiver all the way down to my toes. I panted and whined, but was then silenced when he caught my mouth in a deep kiss.

Pleasure washed over me in waves. I instinctively gave my hips useless little thrusts, trying to push myself harder against him. I was a slave to the motion of his hand.

An instrument just waiting for my strings to be plucked so that I could sing.

A clock ticked somewhere in the bathroom, marking the minutes that passed as Nathan toyed with me.

However, even Nathan's seemingly endless patience had a limit. His hand sped up and he gripped both of us harder, pushing us together toward completion. His kiss turned brutal as he neared his end, as if he were trying to swallow me whole.

I couldn't move, I could barely breathe, and my blood felt like it had turned to fire in my veins.

I loved it.

When I came, I clamped my legs

around his hips, locking him as close as possible to me. He moaned into my mouth as he joined me. Together, the two of us clung tight as we rode out our shared orgasm. Something hot and wet hit my stomach, but I was too overwhelmed to pay it much attention.

So what if my shirt was stained. Everyone probably knew what we'd done anyway. I may as well wear the evidence with pride.

Plus, watching the prudes and homophobes try to hide their disgust would be fun.

When we managed to calm down, and feeling once against returned to my legs, Nathan helped me down from the sink. The damage to my clothing wasn't as bad as I feared, but it still took us a few minutes to get cleaned up and put ourselves back into order.

Nathan finished first. He'd barely removed any clothing, and because he'd been standing over me, gravity had kept him mostly clean. I, on the other hand, had to scrub myself with bathroom paper towels.

"Go on," I told him as I struggled with my pants. "I'll follow you in a minute."

My pants had wormed their way down my thighs while we'd been busy. The tight material was difficult to put on under normal circumstances, but my skin was damp after my hasty clean up, and now my pants refused to budge.

"Are you sure?" Nathan asked as he watched me struggle. The fact that I was losing the fight against my own pants clearly amused him. "I can help."

He reached for me, and I slapped his hand away.

"Oh, no. I know you. Your 'help' will end with me fully naked on this bathroom floor and we'll miss the rest of the party. Shoo. Go shmooze with all the fancy rich people and I'll catch up as soon as I can."

It took some convincing, but he eventually left, and I was alone in the bathroom.

I struggled with my pants for another minute and eventually, succeeded in getting them pulled up after resorting to the jumping technique.

"Finally," I gasped when I pulled up the zipper. "I don't care what Kiki says. I'm never wearing these things again."

The door opened behind me, but I was too busy double checking my clothing to care. During the heat of the moment, I'd thought about walking out of the bathroom wearing the evidence of our tryst, but that was just a fantasy. I didn't actually want people to see me in sex-stained clothes.

"A little slut, aren't you?" someone said behind me.

Before I could turn around to give the stranger a piece of my mind, something hard and cold pressed against the small of my back.

"Shut up and don't say a word," the man spoke directly into my ear.

Unlike with Nathan, there was nothing sexy about his tone.

Looking in the mirror, I got a good look at the man standing directly behind me. He was large in a muscular way, though not unusually so, with a face just handsome enough to be pleasant to look at without drawing too much attention.

It was the kind of face I might give a second glance, but not a third or a fourth.

All of this information filtered through my brain like white noise. None of it mattered. The only thing my attention focused on was the gun pointed at my back.

"What the hell are you doing?" I demanded.

Faster than I could see, the butt of his gun struck the back of my head.

"I said, shut up. Now, come with me. My boss wants a word."

The blow left me dizzy, but not seriously hurt. My vision blurred for a moment, but quickly cleared as the man marched me out of the bathroom, always keeping his gun trained on my back.

Outside, the hallway was empty. Off to my left, the noise of the after-party echoed off the walls. For one moment, I considered calling for help. Surely, if I screamed loud enough, someone would hear, and Nathan would realize I was in trouble.

But what if it wasn't enough?

With so many people in one room, their voices could even drown out a gunshot. Not to mention the music playing over everything. Even if I shouted at the top of my lungs, the guests in the ballroom probably wouldn't hear me, and I would enrage my kidnapper for nothing.

Uncertainty kept me silent, and I was herded off to the right, away from ballroom.

I thought my kidnapper would take me out of the hotel, whisking me off into some lethal unknown. Instead, they dragged me over to the hotel's service elevator. My kidnapper hit the button for the top floor, and the doors closed behind us with a cheery little ding. The gun digging into the small of my back dissuaded me from causing any problems as we waited for the ride to end, though I didn't need the reminder. I wasn't stupid enough to think I could fight a professional criminal, and even if I could, there was nowhere for me to go trapped inside a metal box.

On the thirty-sixth floor, the door opened into the penthouse suite. A neutral palette of cream and beige met my eye, with unassuming pictures of flowers acting as the only accent color. I'd never been to the top floor of such a fancy hotel. The Bellagio even put the hotel I'd visited with Nathan to shame.

For a moment, I almost forgot that I had been kidnapped as I looked around, taking in the details. The space was tastefully decorated, but a little boring. For something so expensive, I expected more.

I was quickly reminded of my situation, however, as the gun dug harder against my back, forcing me to walk forward into the room's main sitting area.

My eye was drawn first to the woman standing just off to the side. Caprice Vidales was easy to recognize, but she looked a little different than the last time I saw her. Her black hair was still cut into its usual harsh bob, but it was frazzled, like she hadn't spent as much time as usual styling it into perfection. There were bags under her eyes, which she had applied a thicker layer of makeup over to try and cover, and she stood with an obvious stoop to her posture.

One hand hovered in front of her stomach, as if protecting it. Although I couldn't see it, I had no doubt that there was some heavy bandaging under her clothes. The knife wound to the stomach that Nathan had given her was obviously causing her problems.

Too bad it hadn't killed her.

The vicious thought made me pause.

I'd never been so bloodthirsty before.

In the past, whenever I'd thought about wanting someone dead, it had never been serious. Now, I knew with absolute certainty that if I had a chance to kill Caprice Vidales, I would without hesitation.

Was this Nathan's influence?

Maybe.

It was hard to say. Certainly, my new attitude toward violence had appeared at the same time he entered my life, but I couldn't say for certain that he was the cause. Until recently, I'd never faced a situation where I legitimately feared for my life or the life of someone I cared about.

Kiki and I were bullied growing up. Even when we pretended to date each other, people in our conservative neighborhood could still sense there was something different about us. We'd often faced bullying, but it was rarely more than harsh words. On the rare occasions when the bullying turned physical, the biggest threat had been scrapes and bruises.

Not once growing up had I ever wondered if I would live to see the next day.

So, maybe Nathan had introduced me to a more nonchalant attitude toward violence. Or maybe I'd always been this way and I'd just never been pushed far enough to know this side of myself.

I spent so long staring daggers at Caprice and wishing to spontaneously develop pyrokinesis and set her on fire with my mind, that I forgot everything else in the room. Even my kidnapper was secondary in my thoughts.

Eventually, the room's other occupant grew tired of waiting for me to notice them and not so subtly cleared their throat.

I finally looked away from Caprice and found myself gazing into very familiar eyes.

"Nathan?"

No, wait. The eyes were the same, but the rest of the face was wrong.

What was going on?

CHAPTER SEVENTEEN

Nathan

Almost the moment I stepped back into the ballroom, D'Angelo was right there to greet me with a knowing smile on his face.

"You were in the bathroom a long time. Should I avoid the hors d'oeuvres?"

I grabbed a glass off a nearby serving tray, not even looking at what it held. "Don't look so smug. I know the kinds of things you get up to. A hotel bathroom is practically classy in comparison."

D'Angelo grabbed the glass out of my hand. "Don't drink the red. I don't know what vintage the hotel claims it is, but they're lying. I've had boxed wine that's better quality."

I no longer held a drink, but my hand wasn't empty. It held a small, folded piece of paper and an even smaller box, no bigger than a coin. Since D'Angelo had gone to such lengths to hand these things to me secretly, I didn't ask him about them. Just raised one eyebrow in a silent question.

"You know," he said causally as he set the untouched glass of red wine on a random side table. "I've been meaning to ask... Where did you find that Vicuna fabric? It's so hard to locate places that produce it."

The paper and box were both so small, yet as I realized what D'Angelo was hinting at, they seemed to suddenly weigh a hundred kilograms.

Or two hundred and twenty pounds, based on American measurements.

I'd asked D'Angelo to figure out which labs were capable of producing the pyrenic that had been used to poison the Vicuna fabric I'd gifted to Deacon. This wasn't something we should be talking about in public where anyone could hear us. For D'Angelo to go through the risk of bringing me this list now, rather than waiting until we were secure in my office, then there must be something on the list I needed to see right away.

I pulled out my phone, holding it in the same hand as the paper.

"I know a guy who deals in rare textiles. I'll give you his number."

As I pretended to type out a text to D'Angelo, I snuck a look at the paper. It held a list of only five labs. Two of them belonged to D'Angelo, just as he'd said, and two of them belonged to people I was certain wouldn't work with Caprice under any circumstances.

The fifth lab on the list, however, was a surprise.

As soon as I saw it, I knew why D'Angelo had brought it to me right away.

D'Angelo pretended to check his phone, as if I had really texted him, while passing me a small nod.

"Thanks. I hope you don't mind, but I'm going to head out. I love parties, but I know nothing about fashion. This isn't really my scene."

He departed almost as abruptly as he'd appeared, leaving me to deal with the new crisis he'd dumped on me.

I almost wanted to hate him for bringing this to my attention, but I couldn't. It was something I needed to know.

After he left, I checked the contents of the small box. The latch was so miniscule, I could barely wedge my fingernail under it to pry it open. Inside, the box held a single red pill. I'd seen it only once before, and was surprised D'Angelo was able to procure it for me so quickly.

Based on the way the night was going, I was going to need the pill sooner than expected.

The box was stored carefully in my pocket, while the paper was unceremoniously thrown away without a second glance. I didn't need to see it again. The names on the list still hovered in my mind like a phantom.

The fifth lab on the list was one I knew, because it was one of my own.

Specifically, it was a lab run by my own organization. My suspicions were confirmed. There was a traitor right under my nose.

I scanned the crowd looking for Deacon. He should have been back already. When I didn't immediately see him, worry gnawed at my gut.

"Lose something?"

Agent Belden's voice grated on my nerves more than usual, like sharp cat's claws dragging along my spine.

It was a miracle I didn't flinch as I turned to face her.

"Agent. I'm happy to say no one has been murdered this time, which means you can't be here in a professional capacity. So, it must be personal. Are you a fan of fashion design?"

My flippant tone clearly annoyed her, and for a moment, I saw her hand twitch toward her gun.

Surely, she wasn't going to draw a weapon in the crowded ballroom. With so many people around, even if there wasn't a single bullet fired, someone was bound to get hurt. Crowds were dangerous things when people started panicking.

Before her hand made contact with her gun, she crossed her arms instead. "I don't waste my time with frivolous things."

"Oh." I shook my head sadly at her. "But frivolous things can be the most fun."

"Does your little pet know that? He

seemed very serious about you. Pity you don't return that commitment, but then I'm not surprised. It's in your nature to sacrifice anything that isn't useful for you anymore, and the poor thing's usefulness seems to have run its course."

I grabbed her arm hard enough that I could feel the outline of muscle under her clothes.

"What are you talking about? What have you done to Deacon?"

Something bad had happened to him. I could feel it, like a sixth sense crawling up the back of my neck. It wasn't a surprise. I had enough enemies that someone was bound to target him as soon as they realized he was important to me. I just hadn't expected Agent Belden to be the one to act first. As a member of law enforcement, harming civilians should be out of bounds for her.

Perhaps, now that Deacon had committed a crime, she no longer saw him as an innocent bystander. There was no evidence proving that Deacon killed anyone, but there was no evidence of my own crimes either, and she was still certain of my guilt.

Agent Belden didn't try to pull away

from my grip and looked me up and down with a critical eye.

"Perhaps he hasn't lived out his usefulness after all. If you want him back, here." She pulled a hotel key out of her pocket and handed it to me. "Although, I would hurry. He was fine last I checked, but there's no telling how long that will last."

My teeth ground together so hard that my jaw ached, but I didn't dare voice my thoughts at that moment. I contented myself with imagining all the painful ways I could kill her as I took the hotel key.

It was for the Bellagio's penthouse.

Turning so quickly I probably left a friction burn in the carpet, I shouldered my way through the crowd, back through the door, and out into the hall. It was an infuriatingly long ride up to the hotel's top floor, especially since Agent Belden insisted on joining me in the elevator. My own security was posted all over the building, but I didn't bother to tell any of them where I was going or what I was doing. They were professionals and didn't need me to micromanage them.

Besides, they probably wouldn't be much help this time.

I tapped my fingers restlessly against my crossed arms as I waited for the elevator to finish its assent. Barely two feet away, I could feel Agent Belden watching me, taking obvious delight in my agitation.

I resisted the urge to roll my eyes.

If the person waiting for me at the top of the hotel was who I thought they were, then things weren't going to end well for her. Unfortunately, the agent was too wrapped up in her obsession with me to see the wolf's den that she'd walked into. I almost felt sorry for her, but there was no room inside me for any other emotions. The worry and anger I felt over the threat to Deacon consumed every last drop of my emotional tolerance.

At the top of the elevator, I was met with more security. Not my own personal security, but faces I recognized.

With rage burning through my veins, I swiped the key over the lock to the penthouse and practically kicked the door open as soon as the light turned green. Inside the penthouse, I found exactly what I expected, but that didn't make the bitter pill any easier to swallow. Even more security stood around the room and

Caprice loitered off to one side, unfortunately still alive.

The security approached me, reaching toward the gun hidden under my jacket.

I grabbed their wrist before they could get close. "Touch me. See what happens."

"Leave him be," another voice said. The security left me alone, and I tugged my jacket back into place.

"What's the meaning of this, Zaur?"

In the penthouse's living room, my brother sat in a plush chair like a king holding court. He'd always had a grandiose way of carrying himself that made me laugh, except this time I didn't find it so humorous.

Not when Deacon was kneeling on the floor at my brother's feet.

Zaur smiled that same wolf-smile we'd both inherited from our father. "K—"

I cut him off.

"Nathan."

"Right," he sighed. "Nathan. How plebeian."

"Don't act like you aren't used to it. I've been going by Nathan Sterling for more than twenty years."

"Yes, but that doesn't mean I like it."

He rolled his eyes at me, and I had to

look away before I smacked him. Instead, I turned my attention toward Deacon. He seemed unharmed, just unhappy, but I had to be sure.

"Deke, are you all right?"

No matter how confused or upset Deacon was, my little spitfire could never be contained. He sat as arrogantly as he could on his knees with his hands bound behind his back, almost looking like he'd chosen to be there.

"I've got a goose-egg on the back of my head that's giving me a migraine, but overall, not bad." Hazel eyes flickered with uncertainty between me and Zaur, no doubt noticing the similarities in our appearance. "So, um, what's going on?"

"How many times do I have to tell you to shut up," one of Zaur's lackeys grabbed Deacon's shoulder and forced him to bow forward until his forehead almost touched the floor. "Next time you speak, I'm putting a bullet in your skull."

The sound of my gun cocking echoed through the room and drew everyone's attention.

"Do it and you won't be leaving this room alive."

I'd drawn my weapon faster than

anyone could react, and it sat in my hand ready to fire. For now, I kept it pointed at the floor, but the promise of violence remained.

Agent Belden stepped up next to me, though she was at least smart enough not to try and grab my gun.

"Are you still throwing around threats even now? You're in over your head this time, Sterling. You've brought too much attention down on yourself, so your boss made us a deal. He's handing you over."

Her smile could have rivaled a kid on Christmas morning, except it was so much crueler.

"I told you I'd see you behind bars one day, even if it means making a deal with the devil himself."

My gaze darted between everyone in the room.

Agent Belden.

Caprice.

The numerous bodyguards and flunkies.

Deacon.

Lastly, it landed on Zaur.

Before anyone could stop me, I stormed over to my brother and grabbed him by the ear.

"You brat. What have you been up to?"

"Ow. Ow. Stop. Let go." He batted ineffectually at my hand. "What? People are supposed to think I'm in charge. That's the whole point, right?"

"Yes." I twisted his ear hard enough to shake his whole head, waiting until his flesh turned a painful red, then let him go. "But it seems like you're starting to believe it as well. What is this nonsense? Secret dealings with the Vidales family I could almost understand. But Interpol? You're trying to bring the law down on me?"

Zaur didn't answer, just rubbed at his abused ear, and scowled at me like a chastised child.

I could feel the weight of so many shocked expressions as everyone in the room stared wide-eyed at me. I didn't have the time or the patience to deal with them, so instead, I knelt beside Deacon and untied him.

"Sorry about this. I didn't realize things had gotten so out of hand."

Deacon massaged his wrists and gently touched the back of his head. "It's fine. I'm— Ow!" He flinched when his fingers made contact with the back of his skull.

Pulling his hand away, I checked the area for myself. There was a tender spot on the back of his head where he'd obviously been struck, and a small cut to his scalp oozed crimson. It was a small wound, less than half an inch long, and wouldn't require stitches, but the sight of Deacon's blood still made me snarl with anger.

Glaring over my shoulder, I caught the eye of the man who had forced Deacon to bow earlier. He was one of Zaur's favorite lackeys and the man was used to a certain level of privilege. However, he now seemed to sense that his privilege didn't extend as far as he thought, and his gaze shifted toward the floor in a show of submission.

"So let me get this straight," Deacon said, unconcerned by the wound on the back of his head. "This guy," he pointed toward Zaur. "Is the leader of the Chechen Mafia. But, not really, because you..." His finger swung toward me in accusation. "Are actually in charge."

"I'll explain in a minute," I said as I helped him to his feet. "Let me take care of things here first."

Deacon still didn't look happy, but he at least didn't argue so I was free to address my brother.

"What is this about, Zaur?"

Crossing his arms, Zaur hesitated and refused to look directly at me. The two of us were similar in appearance, which wasn't surprising considering our father's strong bloodline. The biggest difference was our age. He was over a decade younger than me, closer to Deacon's age than my own. To make up for it, he was always trying to make himself appear older with finely tailored clothes and a full beard.

I'd tried to tell him so many times that no matter how he styled himself, his attitude and posture would always give away his age, but he refused to believe me.

It sometimes baffled me that people honestly believed he could lead anything, let alone one of the top Mafia families in the world. He had his uses. Since everyone thought he was the one in charge, he was good at pulling strings. It had come in handy when I needed to get myself and Deacon out of police custody as soon as possible. However, making his own decisions had never been Zaur's strong point. That was why we had agreed to this arrangement in the first place. So, he could enjoy the privileges of power without having to actually bear the weight of leadership.

I didn't say a word, and just continued to stare at him in a silent demand for answers. The tactic had worked when we were children, and it still worked on him now.

In less than a minute, his resistance crumpled.

"I'm tired of being your figurehead."

Other than our ages, one of the other differences between us was our height. I had a few inches on him, and I used them to my advantage as I confronted him.

"So, you want to be the one in charge now?"

"No," he shouted, fists clenched at his sides. "I want you to take your position as the leader properly. No more skulking around in the shadows. You're the one in charge, so you should be the one under everyone's scrutiny. I'm tired of being your middleman and relaying your orders. Relay them yourself."

My laughter bounced around the

penthouse with such a sharp edge, it was a miracle I didn't cut the paint from the walls.

"You spoiled bastard. Have you really grown so lazy that you can't even handle the illusion of leadership anymore?"

"Hold on," Agent Belden cut in, nearly stepping between us. She realized this was a bad idea just in time to stop herself, but still dared to jab a finger into Zaur's shoulder. "We had a deal. You promised to hand Sterling over to me so long as I left your organization alone."

Zaur rolled his eyes again, and this time I almost joined him.

"I lied, obviously."

"You—" she started to argue, but never got further than a single word. For once Zaur and I were on the same page. Zaur pulled out his own gun and we both shot the agent at the same time.

Two bullets hit her square in the chest. She froze, confused about what had just happened.

A drop of ruby red blood seeped from the corner of her mouth. Wiping it away, she stared at the red stain on her fingers for a moment, brow furrowed in concentration. Then, like someone had flipped a switch and turned her off, she dropped dead to the floor.

I gestured at her with my gun, giving Zaur an incredulous look. "Really. You made a deal with Interpol?"

My gaze flickered toward Caprice in the corner of the room, who had stayed unusually silent since I arrived, and the final piece of the mystery slotted into place.

"One of the things I couldn't figure out was how Caprice's hitman managed to poison the cloth I gave Deacon. It was in the custody of someone from our family the whole time." The barrel of my gun waved lazily at my brother, as non-threatening as a loaded gun could be. "You gave them access and helped them try to poison me."

Zaur merely scoffed as he stored his own gun back in its holster. "Please, like you'd actually fall for that. I knew their little trick wouldn't work on you, but it would draw attention to you. I'd hoped that if the authorities came down on you hard enough, you'd give up this whole charade and come take your proper place as the leader."

I almost felt bad for Caprice. No

wonder she was so bold when antagonizing me. She thought she'd made a powerful ally, but instead of a king, she'd found herself in league with the court jester.

"All this just to make me squirm." I sighed and shook my head. "Do I even want to know what false promises you made to the Vidales family."

Zaur started to answer, but before a single sound could leave his mouth, a vase suddenly came flying at him. He managed to raise his arm in time to avoid a serious head wound, but the broken porcelain still managed to leave a few good cuts on his face and hand. He was drenched in water and crumpled flowers, looking absolutely pathetic as he stared in shock at something just behind me.

Deacon came flying past me, wielding a small decorative statue that he'd picked up from somewhere."

"You fucker." He wielded the statue like a club.

I managed to grab Deacon around the waist before he could get close enough to bash my brother's head in, but that didn't stop him from flailing.

"Let me go. I'm gonna fucking kill

him."

Zaur darted to the other side of a nearby couch to put space between him and Deacon. "Nathan. What the hell is wrong with your boy-toy?"

I was just as confused as Zaur for a moment, but as Deacon kept struggling and shouting curses, I heard Kiki's name mentioned.

Right.

Zaur may not have done the poisoning himself, but without his help Caprice never would have even gotten close. In a way, Kiki's brush with death was Zaur's fault.

There was no point in trying to calm Deacon down. He was enraged, and for good reason.

Instead, I just kept a tight hold around his waist and pinned him at my side.

"Your stunt may not have harmed me, Zaur, but there were still casualties. A designer on my payroll was killed, and a close friend of Deacon's was seriously harmed." When I looked down at the seething man in my arms, who looked ready to tear my brother's throat open with his teeth, I couldn't keep the fond look off my face. "He's very protective."

Zaur made a shooing motion with his hand, as if he could chase Deacon away the same way he swatted a fly. "Well, keep your crazy bitch away from me."

My fond expression disappeared and was replaced with a cold glare. "Don't you dare give me orders right now. Not after the stunt you just pulled. Do you remember what happened last time you threw a tantrum like this?"

It was a rhetorical question. We both knew he remembered.

From my pocket, I pulled out the small box with the single red pill that D'Angelo had given me. I still owed the other man for getting me the first pill a few years ago. Creating *Fantaisiste* to compete with Caprice was supposed to pay that debt, but all I'd done was double it.

Luckily, I liked D'Angelo, because it seemed I'd never be free of the man.

As soon as he saw the pill in my hand, Zaur immediately shut up.

I clicked my tongue at him like a disappointed parent.

"Zaur. Zaur. Zaur. What am I going to do with you?"

CHAPTER EIGHTEEN

Deacon

The struggle in Zaur's eyes was apparent for everyone to see as he stared at the small box in Nathan's hand. It was no bigger than a quarter, and didn't look particularly threatening, but Zaur acted as if Nathan had just pointed a loaded missile at him.

"Go ahead," Zaur said, desperately trying to hide the tremor in his voice. "It doesn't matter. You've already forced me to take that shit. A second dose won't make a difference."

One of Nathan's arms was still wrapped around my waist, keeping me from tearing into Zaur like a wild animal. I'll be the first to admit, when people I care about are threatened, I see red and lose all common sense. The hand on my hip gave a brief squeeze, silently asking if I was all right.

Sucking in a deep breath, I patted Nathan's hand and nodded.

He still didn't seem convinced, probably because he could feel how hard I was shaking. Instead of letting me go, Nathan kept one arm around me and handed me the little box.

"Deke? Do you mind?"

I accepted the box, always keeping one eye on Zaur. The man was now staring at me with as much fear as he'd directed toward Nathan.

The box was even smaller than I thought, and extremely fiddly. I nearly dropped it as I struggled to slip my nail under the latch. When I finally got it open, I found a single red pill inside. Carefully pinching it between two fingers, I held it up to the light for everyone to see. The round, slightly iridescent surface made it look like a bloody pearl.

"What is this?"

"It doesn't have a name." Nathan took

the pill from me with the same gentle firmness as the arm around my waist. "As far as the rest of the world is concerned, it doesn't exist. Only one of these pills is ever made at a time, and it's the most expensive thing I've ever bought."

"Okaaay." I eyed the pill with confusion. "But what does it do?"

Nathan looked like he was about to answer, but then he stopped and turned to his brother. "Zaur? Do you want to answer that?"

With a deep sigh, Zaur turned his head away and refused to look at anyone else in the room.

"It's a paralytic. Anyone who takes it will lose complete control of their body. They'll still be able to breathe, but they won't be able to move at all. Even their vocal cords will be affected, so they'll be mute as well."

He flinched just from recounting the symptoms, and I was certain he knew about the drug from personal experience.

Nathan's arm slid up from my waist to circle around my shoulders. "To put it more poetically, it's a way to imprison someone within their own body." He then gave Zaur a very pointed look, which made the other man flinch again. "This isn't the first tantrum my brother has thrown. A few years ago, I decided I needed a better way to keep him in line, so I slipped him this pill. There's an antidote, but it only works for a month at a time, and the recipe is a heavily guarded secret. If Zaur wants to keep walking around freely, he has to do what I say."

Zaur's hands were balled into fists at his sides, clenched so tightly I could see a drop of blood leaking between his fingers. "Bastard," he hissed under his breath, though not quite enough to go unheard.

Nathan just laughed. "That insult doesn't work on me, Zaur. We have the same parents."

Zaur's lips pulled back to reveal his teeth in a poor imitation of Nathan's intimidating snarl. "One of these days I'm going to find the recipe for that antidote, and then you're going to pay for this."

"But today is not that day." Nathan held the pill up again, presenting it to the eyes of everyone in the room. "However, you are right about one thing. There's no point giving this to you again. A second pill has no more effect than the first. This was just a reminder."

He turned, bringing me with him, so we both faced Caprice Vidales. She still stood in the corner of the room, looking like a lost tourist in a foreign country with only her single personal bodyguard for support.

"What?" Caprice gasped when she realized Nathan's implication. "No. You can't do that."

Nathan finally released me, but he didn't go far as he stalked a few steps closer to Caprice.

"You've been a thorn in my side for too long and gotten too bold. You need to be controlled, for your own sake as well as mine."

"No," she shouted and backed away until she hit a wall. "Just kill me if you dare."

Shaking his head, Nathan tutted at her like he was scolding a child. "No. If I kill you then someone else will just take your place, and nothing will change. This will be much more effective."

I squirmed where I stood, hoping no one was paying attention to me. Something about Nathan's condescending attitude was activating a kink I didn't know I had. It would be different if he spoke to me that way. I could never find such humiliation sexy.

Watching him humiliate other people that I despised was a different matter. My blood ran hot through my veins and a familiar excitement twisted in my gut.

It hadn't even been an hour since our rendezvous in the bathroom downstairs, but my hormones didn't seem to have gotten the message. They were screaming at me as if I were a desperate virgin who'd never known the touch of a man before.

I would definitely be getting Nathan alone as soon as possible.

Nathan ordered Caprice to be captured. There was a moment of confusion where the various bodyguards stationed around the room weren't sure whether to obey or not. With both their figurehead leader and their real leader in the room, the chain of command was a bit muddled. However, Zaur solved the problem by supporting Nathan's order. He seemed relieved that Nathan's attention was off him for now, and happy to throw Caprice to the jaws of The Wolf.

Caprice's lone bodyguard put up a valiant fight. It was the same woman who had guarded her before and managed to survive going toe-to-toe with Nathan.

Unfortunately, she was significantly outnumbered, and Caprice was still injured, so the other woman wasn't much help. The bodyguard was soon restrained, and Caprice was forced to kneel on the ground in front of Nathan. Multiple hands held up her head and pried open her mouth for Nathan to slip the pill inside. He pushed the pill so far down her throat that she gagged, then held her mouth closed to ensure she didn't try to cough it back up.

I was reminded of a dog my family had when I was a child. One time the poor thing got sick, and it was too smart to be tricked by medicine inside treats. So, we'd been forced to shove the pill down the dog's throat each day until it got better.

Nathan handled Caprice in almost the same way, but there were no whispered words of "good girl," and no treat as a reward at the end. Once he was certain she had swallowed the pill, he shoved her away as if touching her skin burned him.

Still kneeling on the floor, Caprice coughed and sputtered until spit dripped down her chin, stained pink from her lipstick. Her hands were held behind her back so she couldn't shove a finger down her throat to try and make herself throw up.

"Bastard," she managed to choke out.

Nathan's arm returned to its place around my shoulders. "Now, unlike my brother, you do have the right to use that insult for me. Although, it's still inaccurate. My parents were married."

Another coughing fit hit Caprice so hard, she doubled over until her forehead touched the floor. Once she managed to regain control of herself, her eyes were watering so badly it smudged her mascara, making her look like she was crying black tears.

"So, what? Now I have to submit myself to you every month for the antidote?"

One of Nathan's hands idly ran through my hair, and I pressed closer to him.

"Oh, no. I'm handing you over to the Bianchi family. You can go to D'Angelo for the antidote, and he'll decide what he wants to do with you."

Caprice gaped up at us, clearly even more horrified by this new information than she had been by her initial poisoning.

I could almost understand. There was some honor in submitting to someone who had bested you. But to be outdone by someone only to be immediately tossed aside was an insult on top of injury.

"Hey, Nathan." I wrapped my arms around him and angled myself against his body so he could feel how hard I was inside my too-tight pants. "Are we done here? I'm... bored."

He laughed with a dark, wicked tone. Yet, the kiss he pressed to my lips was as sweet and light as spun sugar.

"Forgive me. We'll have to take care of your... *boredom* right away."

He led me out of the room, but just before we reached the door that led to the hotel's hallway, a strange sound came from behind us. It sounded like the wail of a dying animal. Looking back, I saw Caprice collapse into a heap on the floor, trembling so bad that she seemed to be vibrating.

"Oh, did I forget to explain," Nathan said as he watched her with a dispassionate gaze. "The initial dose can be rather unpleasant when it takes root.

But don't worry. It won't kill you."

With her hair fallen in disarray over her face, only one eye was visible as Caprice glared up at Nathan from the floor. Fire burned in the depths of her contracted pupil, and her breathing was ragged as she screamed.

No words escaped her. Just incoherent sounds of rage and pain. Her screams followed us as we left the hotel room behind and faded from our ears the moment the door closed.

The elevator ride back down to the first floor passed in a blur as Nathan and I locked in a heated kiss with our hands groping under each other's clothes.

"You know," I gasped as he palmed one globe of my ass and squeezed. "This is a hotel. There's plenty of beds we could use."

I was proud of myself when Nathan grabbed my ass with his other hand and I didn't flinch. Our efforts in bed had been paying off. Maybe I could finally give Nathan the only piece of my virginity that remained.

Nathan never stopped kissing me and spoke in the brief pauses we needed to breathe. "No. Not here. I've got better plans for you."

Unfortunately, we had to part when we reached the ground floor of the hotel. Stepping off the elevator, I was stunned to hear the sounds of the party still taking place in the ballroom. People were laughing, drinking, and even dancing with no idea of what had just taken place above their heads.

And they would probably never know. Based on the efficiency I'd seen from Nathan before, not a word of what had happened in the penthouse would ever reach public ears. Even most law enforcement would probably be left in the dark.

Although my pants technically had pockets, they were too small and tight to actually carry anything, so I'd stashed my phone in Kiki's purse. This was usually fine, except in situations where she was the one I needed to call. Instead, I asked Nathan for his phone and punched in Kiki's number, which I thankfully remembered. I shot her a quick text to explain where I'd gone.

A censored version, of course. I still hadn't told her the truth about Nathan. That was something to tackle later. Now wasn't the time. I would let her enjoy the party in peace and then worry about how to explain everything.

Only seconds after I sent the text, I got a thumbs up emoji in response, letting me know she'd seen my message. Then I returned Nathan's phone and wrapped my arms around his neck.

"All right. Take me away. I want to know what these plans of yours are."

CHAPTER NINETEEN

Deacon

Nathan's plans turned out to be a bubble bath. I'd been longing for one earlier, but after everything that happened in the penthouse, I'd forgotten about it. That desire returned with a vengeance the moment I saw the huge, claw foot tub filled with steaming water and clouds of bubbles just waiting for me to hop in.

Nathan's private apartment was a strange mix of simple and grand. The apartment held only as much as it needed.

A single bedroom.

A small office space.

A single couch.

A single table.

There was even a single set of dishes in the kitchen.

Yet, everything that the apartment did have was luxurious and opulent. Nathan didn't have more than necessary, but he always chose the best option for the things he did need.

The bathroom was no exception. It was just large enough to have a separate tub and shower, but the small space was outfitted with enough white marble and gold to befit a king.

Sitting in that bathtub, I certainly felt like pampered royalty. I was engulfed in hot water and bubbles, with Nathan's arms wrapped around me as he lounged in the bath behind me.

I traced my fingers over one of the tattoos on the back of his hand. He'd explained some of their meanings to me. Predatory animals represented enemies that had left a mark on him, while prey animals represented innocent people whose death he felt responsible for. Weapons represented conflicts that he'd overcome, while flowers were used to represent more abstract concepts he didn't want to forget.

Whenever stars showed up on his skin, they always formed the specific pattern of a constellation. The one on the back of his hand was Cassiopeia, and I'd spotted Eridanus near his collarbone before.

There was still a lot I didn't know about Nathan, such as the meaning behind these two constellations. In fact, there was a lot I didn't know in general about life among the Mafia and how the criminal underworld operated.

"Hey, Nathan?"

He gave a non-committal noise of acknowledgement from behind me, limp and relaxed in the water.

"What's going to happen to that agent?"

"Hmm?" He raised his head from where it had been leaning back against the rim of the tub.

"From Interpol. Agent Belden. What's going to happen with her? I assume you want to cover up the fact that you and your brother killed her, but an Interpol agent can't just disappear. People will notice. So, what's the plan?"

Nathan let his head fall back against the rim of the tub and threaded his fingers between mine.

"Her body will be taken somewhere else and staged to look like the victim of a mugging, or something similar."

"But won't it look suspicious that she disappeared while investigating you? Even if her body is found somewhere else?"

"Yes, it would, if she were actually investigating me."

Water sloshed around in the tub as I turned to face him, straddling his lap when my legs had nowhere else to go. "What do you mean?"

His hands found my thighs under the water and started stroking along my skin.

"Interpol is an international law enforcement agency. There was no reason for them to be investigating any of these recent incidents. Even the model who was killed at your first show. She turned out to be the FBI director's niece, but that still isn't an international affair."

I leaned into him until our chests pressed flush together and my nose was buried against his neck.

"So, you're saying Interpol wasn't supposed to be involved."

His hands dug a little harder into my flesh. "Interpol wasn't there. Agent Belden was acting off the books to pursue her own agenda against me. Interpol isn't going to want anyone to know that their agent was acting outside of sanctioned orders, so they're going to sweep everything under the rug as quickly as possible. So long as we give them a convenient explanation for her death, they're not going to look any further into it."

I moaned as one of his hands slipped between my legs to grip my arousal, which had calmed down but not fully vanished since leaving the Bellagio. At the same time, his other hand slid around behind me, so his fingers just dipped into the crease of my ass, barely touching the rim of my hole.

The hard line of his body rubbed against me as I squirmed, sending water splashing over the edge of the tub. I bit the shell of his ear in retaliation, but it backfired. The spark of pain from my teeth only excited him, and I felt the heat of his own arousal brush against my stomach.

If he started moaning, I wouldn't be able to control myself. As I'd already established, the sound of his voice was too much of a turn on. To silence him, I captured his mouth in a hungry kiss that would swallow any sound he made.

On instinct, I started grinding my hips, pushing myself harder against his touch. The hand that was wrapped around my cock sped up, and the hand on my ass grew bold enough to start rubbing deliberately around my rim.

Little jolts of pleasure danced along my nerves, and for once, I wasn't nervous at all.

I sighed into the kiss, making my enjoyment known.

Without warning, Nathan suddenly stopped what he was doing and wrapped his arms around me, then stood from the tub. He brought me with him, keeping my legs locked around his waist to help support my weight as he stepped out of the tub and left the bathroom behind. I watched the puddles we left in our wake over Nathan's shoulder. If I looked at the bed, I would probably get nervous again, and I wanted to stay relaxed.

Nathan said he had plans for me, but I had plans, too, and they didn't involve letting my irrational anxiety get the best of me once again.

Nathan's bed was just as luxurious as the rest of the apartment. It was one of the few things that was bigger than it needed to be, a California King, and was draped in blue-gray sheets. The fine silk clung to my damp skin when Nathan deposited me on the bed. They were cool to the touch, as silk always was, and I shivered until Nathan joined me. The heat of his body chased away even the memory of cold.

We tangled tightly together, kissing like we could only breathe air from the other person's lungs. Nathan groped blindly with one hand through the nightstand drawer to pull out a bottle of lube, never once letting our mouths part.

The sound of the cap popping open brought me back to my senses.

"Wait."

Nathan froze, the open bottle still held in one hand.

"What's wrong?"

"Nothing. I just... I want to do something." I held out my hand for the bottle. "Can I?"

Without hesitation, he placed the bottle in my hand.

"Whatever you want. I owe you after

letting you get kidnapped tonight. Even if it was just my brother, you still shouldn't have had to go through that."

Holding the bottle, I nervously toyed with the cap. He sounded so certain, but would his offer remain when he realized what I wanted to do?

Only one way to find out.

"All right. Can you lie down? On your stomach? I want... I want to be in control."

This time there was a moment of hesitation. Last time Nathan submitted himself to me, he'd still been in control, even going so far as to handcuff me to the headboard.

The moment passed, and Nathan seemed to come to a decision with himself. His movements were stiff but certain as he lay down on his stomach with his legs spread just a little.

Running a hand over his back and admiring the ripple of muscles I felt, I leaned in to bite his ear again.

"Thank you."

His crossed arms acted like a pillow as he looked at me over his shoulder. "Don't thank me. Asking for what you want in bed shouldn't be treated like I'm making some great sacrifice for you. If I didn't want to do it, I wouldn't."

He spread his legs wider, making enough room for me to kneel between. There were scars on his back, more so than on his front. The most prominent ones were the slashes over his shoulders, and a particularly gnarled spot where it looked like someone had tried to stab him in the kidney. The worst scars were old and had faded to a pale silver color. The few young, pink scars were small and seemed to be the result of superficial wounds, rather than anything life-threatening.

He had tattoos on his back as well, and when a scar distorted the artwork, it was left that way. There had been no effort to correct the tattoos or hide the scars. Although Nathan had never said so out loud, I was certain that he considered the combination of scars and tattoos like a storybook mapping out his life. Every accomplishment and failure was etched into his skin one way or another so they would never be forgotten.

Would I ever appear on his skin?

I took a moment to trace each scar and tattoo, committing them to memory as I made my way down his back. His ass was firm, with just as much muscle as the rest of his body, and I couldn't resist the urge to sink my teeth into the top of the swell just below his left hip-dimple.

"Did you just bite me?" he asked over his shoulder, though he didn't try to pull away.

My teeth left a slight mark but didn't break the skin. "Problem?"

He laughed. It was an awkward, breathy sound that people made when they didn't know what else to do. "No, just... no one's ever dared to do that before."

I bit him again, on the right side this time for the sake of symmetry. "You should know by now, I like the thrill of living on the edge."

Having reached my destination, there was no more time to delay. "Squeezing out a generous amount of lube, I pressed one finger inside him.

I'd literally fucked this man before. Yet, somehow, gently fingering him open was a million times more intimate than sex. Every moan and every twitch were on full display. It made finding his sweet spots even easier. All I had to do was listen for the hitch in his breath and I knew I'd hit my target.

By the time I had three fingers inside him, he was growling low under his breath and practically tearing at the pillow beneath him.

"Are you just going to toy with me all day, or are you going to get on with it?"

Leaning forward so I stretched over his back, I pressed a kiss just behind his ear. "Patience. Let me have my fun."

Although I said that, I was eager to continue as well. My throat had gone dry, and my belly trembled in anticipation.

Kneeling behind him, I gripped his hips, lined myself up, and slowly pressed inside.

Even with my preparation, he was tighter than he'd been before. I wasn't sure if it was the different angle, or if he was nervous from being in such a submissive position, but his inner walls gripped me like a vice.

I gasped and my hands shook on his hips, but I didn't stop. As soon as I was as deep as I could go inside him, I paused to regain some control over myself. I could already tell I wasn't going to last long.

Thankfully, I managed not to

embarrass myself by coming the moment I started moving. I slammed my hips against him, harder than I originally intended. Based on the sounds he was making, he didn't mind.

I managed to last about a minute with him squeezing so tightly around me. Once I'd started, I couldn't stop, and I chased my own pleasure like I was running full speed off the edge of a cliff.

Wrapping my arms around him, I pressed myself flush to his back and buried my face against his neck when I came. Every muscle in my body locked into place as white-hot ecstasy crashed through me in waves. The orgasm was short, but intense, and left me gasping for air when it faded.

Throughout it all, Nathan didn't move. It was clear he hadn't found his own end, but he remained relaxed and submitted to me, letting me take as much as I wanted from him.

"Thanks," I whispered against his ear when I found my voice again. "That was great."

I pulled out and moved to the side, so I was lying next to him.

His hand automatically landed on my

hip, keeping me close as he rolled over to face me. "I wouldn't do that for anyone else, you know. The few times I've let someone top me, I've never given up control like that."

"I know." I pressed a quick, sweet kiss to his lips. "That's why... I think I can finally do this."

I didn't bother to say more, and let my actions speak for themselves. Laying flat on my back with my hands up by my shoulders, I raised my knees and let my legs fall open in an obvious suggestion.

"Really?" He sounded eager, but he was still gentle as he slowly positioned himself between my legs. "You're certain you're ready?"

Biting my lip to keep any nervous words at bay, I nodded. "Yes. I've trusted you with literally everything else. My life. My health. My career. My friends. There's no reason I can't trust you with this as well."

As his weight settled against me, I trembled. I tried to tell myself that it was from anticipation, but I was lying. Anticipation certainly existed, I was definitely eager, but my gut also twisted in an unpleasant way. Previous experiences with past lovers flashed behind my eyes, and I kept my gaze locked on Nathan.

I knew this man. I trusted him. So long as I kept reminding myself who was currently pushing my knees even farther apart, I would be fine.

When his slicked fingers probed at my ass, I buried both my hands under the pillow behind my head to keep them still. I even clenched my toes in the sheets to make sure I didn't accidentally kick him.

This was fine.

We'd done this before.

The feel of his fingers sliding inside me was familiar, and it took little effort for me to relax and enjoy his attention.

However, the preparation process only lasted so long, even with Nathan taking his time. Soon enough, my body was ready for him, and I could feel the hot press of his cock against my ass.

"Ready?" Nathan asked me. He was visibly trembling with the effort of holding back.

It should have been intimidating, knowing how dangerous Nathan could be and how close he was to snapping. Yet, I was also completely certain that he wouldn't move forward until I gave the okay. If I told him "No" right now he would stop without a word of complaint.

That certainty gave me the courage to take a deep breath and finally say what I'd never been able to say to any other partner before.

"Do it. I want you."

After experiencing the slide of his fingers inside me, I expected his cock to feel similar. It was the same act, after all, just with something slightly larger.

I was wrong.

The moment the head of his cock forced its way passed the rim of my hole, I was overcome with an electric sensation running up and down my body. It reached from my toes all the way to the crown of my head. I felt so many different sensations at once, I couldn't even tell if it counted as pleasure or not.

It was all just so much.

"Please. Na— ah! Nathan. I don't... Fuck!"

His cock slid in deeper, slowly, inch by inch. I gasped and squirmed as I was claimed properly for the first time. Nathan held me the whole time, arms wrapped tight around me, so I was surrounded by him in all directions. I clung to him, my nails digging into his back as I trembled and panted.

Finally, he was fully buried inside me, and I swore I could feel him all the way in my stomach. For a moment, I worried that he would pause just like I had. If he stopped in that moment, it would only give my brain time to think, and I feared I would panic.

Maybe I babbled my fears out loud, or maybe he was just that in tune with me, but Nathan didn't hesitate. He immediately pulled back to slowly slide out. Then, when only the head of his shaft remained inside, he thrust in faster than before, starting a strong rhythmic pace. His thrusts sped up gradually, giving me time to adjust, until he was properly fucking me.

My whole body jolted each time he slammed back inside, forcing the air out of my lungs and causing me to make a bunch of embarrassing little sounds. On one particularly deep thrust, he hit a spot inside me that made my whole vision go white and a long moan tumbled from my throat. I knew that spot was there. Nathan had toyed with it before. Yet, having it struck in such a way while being stretched open to my limit at the same time was so much more intense.

It was like we were made to fit together. Each time his cock plunged inside me, it hit all of my best spots at the same time, and when it pulled out it tugged at my rim in a way that made me want more.

Although I'd just come a few minutes ago, I was filled with such ecstasy that my own cock was standing hard once again. I was lost to a haze of sensation, and I had no idea how long Nathan kept at it, rewriting me from the inside until I was certain that I would never fit anyone else but him.

I regained some sense of myself when Nathan's pace changed. He sped up and pushed even deeper. I couldn't speak. Couldn't even moan. Tears dripped from my eyes, but I didn't bother brushing them away. My hands were too busy tangling in his hair.

"Come on. Take me. Let me feel it."

He sped up even faster and I pulled him into a kiss. We moaned against each other's mouths as we came at the same time.

Heat flooded me inside and out, and I clung to Nathan until my fingers went numb. He was also breathing heavily. His chest heaved against mine and his breath fluttered against my skin. The pleasure of climax slowly drifted away, leaving us lethargic and practically melted together.

"Fuck," I groaned. "That was... Why haven't we done that sooner?"

Nathan held me tighter, still trembling with the aftershock of our shared pleasure. "You weren't ready yet."

"I know," I sighed, before pressing a few kisses down his chest, right over the ink that decorated his skin. "Well, now that I know how good it can be, you better be prepared. I'm going to want you to fuck me all the time."

With a groan, Nathan sat up enough to look down at me properly. "I've never had someone threaten me with sex. Today is certainly a day of firsts."

Scowling up at him, I poked him just under his rib cage, hoping to see him squirm. "I mean it. You had better be prepared. I can get very obsessive when I desire something."

He silenced me with another kiss, but it only lasted a moment before his lips traveled to my ear. "So long as the thing you desire is me, then feel free to obsess as much as you want." He spoke directly into my ear in that way he knew turned me on. I shivered, and if I wasn't already so exhausted, I would have gotten hard again.

Eventually, Nathan carefully extracted himself from me and rolled off to the side, so he no longer hovered over me. I felt cold and strangely empty when he was gone, and I held tight to whatever part of him I could reach.

I was also a mess, but I tried not to think about that. No reason to spoil the moment.

We rearranged ourselves so Nathan sat against the headboard, and I was in the circle of his arms with my back to his chest. His fingers drew idle designs against my skin, and I was halfway asleep when his voice rumbled in my ear.

"Hey, Deke. I want to hire you for something."

"What?" I asked blearily. "We literally just finished creating a new fashion line and you already want another one?"

"No, not that." His hand fell still and pressed against my chest right over my heart. "I want you to design a tattoo for me."

My fatigue instantly vanished and I spun around to face him. "What? A tattoo? You mean, like... for you?"

He already had so many, but my gaze instantly found the bare patches of skin still available. One spot on his chest caught my eye. It wasn't too large, but it was near his heart, exactly where I'd leave my mark if given the choice.

Nathan ran a hand over himself, all the way from neck to stomach. "Yes. I want something of yours on my skin so I can always carry it with me. So, what'd you say? Design me something?"

Words eluded me as I jumped up from the bed to fetch something to draw with. I probably looked like a fool, rummaging through an apartment that I didn't know for drawing supplies.

Eventually, I found some paper and a pen in the home office—where I probably should have checked first—and ran back to the bedroom.

Nathan hadn't moved from where I left him. He laughed at me as I threw myself back into his arms and curled up on his lap so he could see the paper as well. My mind was already flooded with so many ideas and it seemed like my fingers couldn't move fast enough as I started to draw.

I had no idea what the final tattoo would look like, just as I had no idea where my relationship with Nathan would go in the future. However, tattoos were permanent, and I considered it a good sign. No matter what happened in the future, and no matter what direction our relationship took, Nathan and I would be a permanent fixture in each other's lives.

Dear Reader,

Thank you for reading Kissing Danger, book three in the Ruthless Empire series.

If you enjoyed this taste of morally gray alpha men who live and die by family loyalties and honor, and will unalive anyone who touches their man, please let me know.

You can simply return to the online retailer where you made your purchase and leave me a short review. Your thoughts may just encourage other readers to try my books, and help me continue writing the bad boys we all love. Even a few words means the world to me.

I may just find more ways to sweep you

off to the underground world of the brutal lives of mafia men and their prospective life partners. Filled with dangerous deeds and plenty of smexy times, too, of course. ☺

~Love, Evie Riley

OTHER BOOKS BY EVIE

Federal Protection Agency
Mason
Rafe
Ryzen
Cooper
Noah
Damien
Sebastian
Gabe
Logan

Ruthless Empire
Courting Danger
Chasing Danger
Kissing Danger

Smokejumpers
Hawke
Cyrus
Jase
Gage
Jackson
Xavier

Jasper Springs
Cade
Dawson
Drew
Grayson
Riley
Mitch

From The Edge
Shattered
Runaway
Jaded
Rescue
Hidden
Tormented

Gray Vale Pack
His Fated Mate
His Wounded Warrior
His Healing Heart

ABOUT THE AUTHOR

Evie Riley is a prolific, neurodivergent author known for her captivating MM romance novels. She has gained a significant following and topped the LGBT+ action and adventure bestseller charts with her series.

Evie's writing style often explores dark and gritty themes where her men must overcome difficult obstacles in their search for love, but she has also ventured into sweeter small-town romances, incorporating tropes like enemies-to-lovers, friends-to-lovers, age-gap, and forced proximity. She is known for crafting engaging romantic suspense novels and has a knack for creating interconnected series worlds that keep readers invested.

Interestingly, Ms. Riley has hinted at exploring new genres, such as Alien Omegaverse Romance, in the future.

Outside of writing, she enjoys spending time at the beach and has a quirky personality, described by her partner as ranging from cute to deadly, depending on her blood-chocolate levels.

Evie spends her nights writing bad boys in love, and her days wrangling the sweet boys she loves.

www.ingramcontent.com/pod-product-compliance
Lightning Source LLC
Chambersburg PA
CBHW071408200726
48294CB00002B/325